THE DATING RESOLUTION

BY
HANNAH BERNARD

First published in Great Britain 2004
Harlequin Mills & Boon Limited,
Eton House, 18-24 Paradise Road, Richmond, Surrey TW9 1SR

© Hannah Bernard 2004

ISBN 0 263 18341 6

Set in Times Roman 10½ on 12¼ pt.
07-0904-42168

Printed and bound in Great Britain
by Antony Rowe Ltd, Chippenham, Wiltshire

"I never knew I had a weakness for blondes," Jordan mused.

She didn't even manage to draw a breath of relief before his hand dived deeper into her hair, cupping the back of her head, his thumb stroking her scalp. Goosebumps streaked down her back and up again, making her breath catch as she met his eyes. "But maybe I don't," he continued. "Maybe it's just you."

"This is not a good idea," she stammered. "Definitely, absolutely, positively not. In fact, it's a bad idea. A rotten idea."

"It's the best idea I've had all year."

"You know there's no point. It can't go anywhere. Too complicated..."

"We're not getting married," Jordan murmured. Oh, Lord. He was kissing her jaw, close to her ear, his bristly cheek rubbing hers, and her goosebumps got goosebumps. "We're just going to kiss."

Hannah Bernard always knew what she wanted to be when she grew up—a psychologist. After spending an eternity in university, studying towards that goal, she took one look at her hard-earned diploma and thought: Nah. I'd rather be a writer. She has no kids to brag about, no pets to complain about, and only one husband, who any day now will break down and agree to adopt a kitten.

Recent titles by the same author:

THE HONEYMOON PROPOSAL
MISSION: MARRIAGE
THEIR ACCIDENTAL BABY
BABY CHASE

PROLOGUE

BREATHING in the familiar scent of chalk, Hailey squirmed into the small seat behind the dwarfish desk and faced her friend from the perspective of a nine-year-old. "I'd like to make a statement," she announced.

"I'm holding my breath," Ellen managed to say around the pen between her teeth. She pulled a thermos out of her briefcase and filled the yellow plastic cup. "Why can't thermoses ever keep coffee warm more than a couple of hours?" she complained with a grimace after spitting out the pen and taking a sip. "Someone should do something about that."

"This is an important announcement. Put down your coffee and pay attention."

"Sounds serious. Is it about your New Year's resolutions?"

"Of course. What else would it be this time of year?"

Ellen made a show of pushing her coffee away and leaning back in her seat. "Well, let me hear it."

Hailey sat up straight, preparing for her dramatic declaration. "No more men!" she called out, emphasizing it with a sweeping hand gesture.

"Uh-huh," Ellen said, returning her attention to the pile of paper in front of her. "Right. And you're going cold turkey on chocolate too, aren't you?"

"Well—"

5

"…and doing daily sit-ups?"

"Well—"

"And getting up earlier on weekends?"

Hailey frowned. This was the annoying thing about friends. They knew you too well. "This time, I mean it. Seriously. And for more than two weeks."

"I see. Why? Must be pretty urgent since you invaded my classroom to tell me."

Hailey glanced around the third grade classroom, empty of children, but not of children's presence. Classrooms never were. "At least I waited until the kids were gone. Although," she added darkly, "if someone had told me the truth about men at an early age, I could have joined a convent straight out of high school and saved myself a lot of misery."

"You mean you hadn't already figured boys out by third grade?"

"Nope, stars in my eyes until I was nineteen or so. I guess I was a late developer. Hence all the scars on my heart."

"Aw, Hailey." Ellen made a sympathetic sound, but her pen did not pause on the paper she was scribbling on. "Why are you really here?"

"No other reason! I just wanted you to be the first to know. Especially as you're always dragging guys in my direction."

"No more men, huh?"

"No more men. As in, you're not allowed to set me up, introduce me to guys, or in other ways work against my resolution."

"I see. And are you—in principle—swearing off men for good?"

"Well, no," Hailey admitted. "I haven't entirely lost my faith in half of the human race. Not yet."

"Phew."

"It's me. I've been making so many mistakes when it comes to guys. So, I'm taking a year out."

"A year?"

"Yep."

"A whole year?"

"Yes."

Ellen put down her pen and leaned forward. "Hailey, do you have any idea how long a year is?"

"Three hundred and sixty-five days. And don't make me calculate the hours. I'm lousy at multiplication."

"An entire year?"

"Yep. One year. No men. No dates. Nothing. I'm going to pretend the other sex doesn't exist."

Ellen tossed a finished sheet to the side and grabbed the next one. "And—assuming that there is a problem in the first place—how's a year out going to solve anything? You'll be in exactly the same situation after a year has passed."

Hailey tried to get comfortable, but in a chair that size, it was close to impossible. Someone had scribbled a swearword in crayon on the desk, and she rubbed at it with a finger, although she could well echo the sentiment. Maybe third-graders got their hearts trampled on too. "No, I won't. That's the whole point. Think, Ellen. What do our lives revolve around?"

Ellen pushed her glasses up above her forehead, displaying the tiny wrinkles between her eyes as she pondered the question. "Do you mean practically or philosophically?"

"It's not a trick question."

"I don't trust you. With you, everything's a trick question."

"It's simple. What is the one thing we're always thinking about, always talking about?"

"Is this one of your veiled 'What's the meaning of life?' questions?"

"Guys! That's what our life revolves around. Even most of our conversations revolve around guys." Hailey banged her fist on the table in emphasis. "I am *sick* of spending my life sifting through men in search for an elusive—perhaps even mythological—nugget of gold."

Ellen grinned, gesturing with a pencil. "Well, you've got to admit, sifting can be fun even if you don't always strike gold."

Hailey stared over Ellen's shoulder at the chalkboard behind her. "Imagine—all those gold prospectors back then. Spending years, decades, their entire lives, hoping to strike a treasure, sacrificing everything else—home, family. All most of them ever got was disappointment, pain, sweat and tears. Even those few who thought they'd been lucky—so often it turned out to be fool's gold."

Ellen returned her attention to third-grade spelling problems. "It takes an IQ higher than mine to follow your analogies, Hailey, but I'm pretty sure you're being depressing again."

Hailey shook her head. "My point is, why are we doing this?"

Ellen got that annoying dreamy look on her face. "I know the answer to this one. Because true love is somewhere out there waiting for us—only it's a bit hard to find.''

"No. True love is society's myth. Don't you see? We're being sucked into a global lie.''

''I see.'' Ellen sounded rather unconvinced. "Love is a worldwide conspiracy. Are aliens involved?''

"Whether true love exists or not, the truth is that the real reason we subject ourselves to this is because it's expected of us. Because we're considered inferior if we're not part of a couple. We're caving in to social pressure, and for what?''

Ellen opened her mouth, but Hailey barged on, not allowing her to interrupt. She was on a roll. She'd spent her entire miserable, lonely—even in a crowd—New Year's Eve composing this manifesto in her head and Ellen would hear it whether she liked it or not. "Broken hearts, that's what we get for trying! Lousy dates, broken hearts and plummeting self-esteem each time one of the many idiots in the world displays his true colors.'' She leaned toward Ellen and the tiny table creaked alarmingly. "Don't you see? We're not doing this because we *want* to, but to fulfill the role society expects of us. It all comes back down to biology. Despite all our technological advances, modern man—modern *woman*—is still very much a slave of biology when it comes to happiness. When women aren't mothers, they aren't happy unless they are actively engaged in the pursuit of someone to father their child. It's that simple.''

Ellen gave her a wry glance. "I knew it. You've been reading those feminist pseudoscience books again.''

"In a nutshell, my discovery is this…'' She paused

for dramatic emphasis. *"There's nothing wrong with being single."*

Ellen failed to look impressed. All she did was shrug. "As that seems to be our ongoing state, I should hope not."

"But we *feel* there's something wrong with it. It's an instinctive feeling, almost like it's a biological force programmed in our genes. And that's exactly what it is. It *is* biological."

"Good Lord, Hailey! You're overcomplicating things. What's wrong with wanting a partner in life? It's just human."

"Exactly. That's my problem."

"Your problem is being human? Well, welcome to the club."

Hailey looked down and mumbled her next words. "You see, I've discovered something about myself, and I don't like it."

"What is it?"

Hailey took a deep breath before making her confession. "I'm a relationship addict."

"Oh, God, more psychobabble."

"I am!"

"Is that a terminal condition?"

Hailey glared at her friend. "Why do I always confide in you? Zero sympathy. Zero understanding. Worst of all, zero co-dependence. Aren't you supposed to be my best friend?"

"Okay." Ellen started piling stuff into her briefcase. "I'll be good. Tell me about your relationship addiction."

Hailey bit her lip. She probably sounded like she was being flippant about this, but the pain and humiliation of her self-discovery cut deep. "I am not happy unless I am in a relationship."

"Come on! That's not true!"

"It is! This is why I hurry into a relationship before I'm ready, before the guy is ready, before either one of us is sure this is what we want—before we even know each other. Then when we break up—for whatever reason that is—I rush to the next relationship, anxious to do it right *this* time. It's a vicious cycle."

Despite her promise, Ellen was rolling her eyes again. "Come on, Hailey, it's not that dramatic."

"Case in point. Dan. You never trusted him, did you?"

"Well…"

"You knew he was a rat long before I did. Long before I wanted to know. But I was so desperate to have it work out that I ignored all the hints, all the lies and deceit…"

"Love is blind—"

"No! *Love* is not blind. *I'm* blind. And I was on the rebound when I met him, remember? Things weren't much better that time around, either. It's a vicious cycle and I've been stuck in it."

"Hailey, fess up, you've been watching those daytime psychobabble shows, haven't you?"

Hailey crossed her arms on her chest and scowled at her friend. "Fine, fine, make fun of my brilliant theory. But it comes down to this. Will you support me in my decision?"

"A year with no dates?" Ellen shrugged. "Sure. Can't hurt. A year is nothing. I've had longer dry spells than one year. Just make sure you always have plenty of chocolate on hand."

"I've given up chocolate too."

"You can't give up chocolate *and* men, Hailey! That's not a resolution, it's self-torture!"

A good point. "You're right. I'll give up chocolate next year."

Ellen snickered. "So, what happens after the year has passed? How is this going to help?"

Hailey shrugged. "After a year my mind will be clearer. I will have broken free of the cycle. I will be better able to sift through the mud."

"Mud?"

"Men."

"Mud equals men—and you still want one? Something isn't adding up here."

"When I get some distance, I will gain a new perspective. I might be able to tell real gold from fool's gold. Or—" She shrugged. "This is also a possibility—I might have accepted the fact that Mr. Right is nothing but a romantic myth and that I'll be a lot happier if I stop trying to create reality out of a pathetic girlish fantasy."

Ellen grimaced as she pushed the stack of papers away and reached for her coffee cup again. "Ouch. I'd like to stick with fantasy, thank you."

"Why build castles in the air if they're just going to come crashing down on your head? I mean—why would we need a man to the level of being almost desperate for a relationship? We're modern women. We can do anything we want. Right? *Right?*" It was a battle cry, but not surprisingly, it had little effect on Ellen.

"Uh…right."

"Damn right! We can have companionship, friendship, a social life, a career, even children—whatever we want without bringing 'love' into it. We don't need men!''

''Uh…Hailey…remember, that thing men are good for?''

''What?'' Hailey stared at her friend, frowning. ''Oh, *that*. Well, I'll just have to pay for it, I guess.''

Ellen sputtered coffee. *''Pay for it?''*

Hailey raised an eyebrow. ''Fixing roofs and leaking sinks and such, that's what you meant, wasn't it?''

''No.'' Ellen shook her head for emphasis. ''No. That's not what I meant. You know very well that's not what I meant.''

''Maybe I'll just buy myself some tools.''

''Tools?''

Ellen looked intrigued now. When Hailey figured out why, she tilted her head back and looked up at the ceiling with an exaggerated expression of disgust. ''You have such a dirty mind. I mean *tools* tools. You know, for fixing the roof and such.''

''Oh,'' Ellen muttered. ''Okay. Never mind, then.''

''Well, you're right, there are things a woman can use a man for if you want to be old-fashioned and dependent and stick to traditional roles—but he is definitely not *necessary*. I'll just go forth and purchase a cute little toolbox of my very own. I mean, it's not like there's any good reason why I shouldn't be able to fix the roof myself.''

Ellen was looking confused now. ''Which roof are we talking about, anyway?''

''A rhetorical roof.''

Ellen nodded. ''Right. I think I had one of those once. It did leak. But you know, a toolbox isn't going to whisper sweet nothings and cuddle you while you sleep.''

Hailey shook her head. ''The cuddles come at too great a price. This will be great. I'll make new friends, I'll start taking classes and find myself new hobbies, and I can stop worrying about my love life, stop dreading every weekend—whether I have a date or not.'' She leaned on the small desk, gesturing earnestly. ''Over the holidays I started thinking—why am I doing this? Dating makes me miserable. I'm happiest when I take a break from all that. Unfortunately I never get away with it long, before someone has set me up, and I always agree to go, thinking this time it might be different. Why do we do that? Why are we so hung up on this ridiculous idea that there is a perfect guy for us somewhere out there? Where does this true love myth come from?''

''Don't. You're making me depressed.''

''Exactly. Just the thought of there being no Mr. Right has us depressed. So we get desperate and take all kinds of crap, just to avoid the horrible, terrible, paralyzing thought of being still single at thirty. I've had it. I've trusted too many liars, wasted too much time on losers. It stops here.''

''Hailey, you're being ridiculous. Okay, so you've been unlucky with some of your boyfriends...''

Hailey sent her a look.

''Okay, all of your recent boyfriends,'' Ellen amended with a grimace. ''But that doesn't mean there isn't a decent guy for you out there. Somewhere.''

''Ah, the elusive someone somewhere sometime. Maybe mine is in Alpha Centauri, born approximately in the twenty-fifth century?''

Ellen pointed at Hailey with a pencil. "I'm serious. There's someone out there for everyone. More importantly, your bad luck with guys does *not* mean there's something wrong with you."

That was the point, wasn't it? There *was* something wrong with her. Simply a dysfunctional pattern, she hoped, not a personality flaw. Something she could work through, habits she could break. That was what this year was all about. If there was a gold nugget out there, she'd never find it if she kept her nose in the mud simply out of desperation. "I just need some time to myself," she said, her tone low now. "Away from the dating scene. I need a chance to break free from this evil cycle—then I can start afresh."

"Hailey…"

"Don't you see? It's necessary for me to get out of my current dysfunctional pattern. Embrace possibilities. Can-bes instead of must-bes."

Ellen rolled her eyes, but Hailey could nevertheless detect a glow of sympathy and understanding. "I will support you in this, but Hailey, you're *definitely* watching too many talk shows."

CHAPTER ONE

THE house was locked and abandoned. She'd knocked for ages—and then finally resorted to trying the doorknob.

She'd flown halfway across the world—and come to a locked door. Now what? Jane had told her someone would greet her here.

This wasn't a good sign, was it?

Maybe "someone" was simply late. She pushed her suitcases to the side and sat down on the step. Jane wasn't answering her cell phone, so she dug in her purse for the printout of her last e-mail to double check the street name and number. Yes. She was at the right place, and the right time had come and gone twenty minutes ago, but nobody was here yet.

She sent Jane a text message, then stuffed the phone and the diary back into her purse.

She'd wait awhile.

Then she'd panic.

At least the house looked nice. And the street was pretty and quiet—if you didn't count the noise of children yelling. Of course, for a schoolteacher that was mere background noise.

Hailey was so mesmerized watching the children rush back and forth on their bikes in the street that she nearly screamed when a shadow fell over her.

"Sorry. Didn't mean to startle you. You must be Hailey?"

16

She squinted up at him. He looked like a tall and menacing shadow from this angle, but at least the voice wasn't menacing. This was probably ''someone.'' ''Where did you come from?''

''Next door. Jumped over the fence, so you probably didn't see me coming. I'm Jordan Halifax.'' He shifted to the side and she could look at him. Still tall and menacing and scruffy—in what she and her girlfriends in her previous life would have called a *hot* way. ''Jane asked me to check on you when you arrived.''

They made sexy men in Alaska too. Dammit.

But she wasn't seeing sexy. Nope. Not for another five months. See no sexy, hear no sexy, speak no sexy. She squinted until he looked like an undefined shadow again. Safer that way. ''Hi. Jane said someone would meet me here, and I guess you're it.''

''Is there something wrong with your eyes?''

Hailey blinked, and he came into focus again. ''Sorry. It was the sun. Do you have my key?''

''The key? No.''

''What?''

''The key is always under the pot.'' Jordan nodded at a terra-cotta pot next to the door. ''Didn't Jane tell you about it? Just push the flowerpot a bit to the right, and you'll find it.''

Key under a flowerpot? Seriously? What was this, a place out of time?

She pushed at the pot with the heel of her hand. It scraped on the old scarred concrete, but yes, there it lay. A house key. A bit rusty, showing it probably spent most of its time outdoors.

Jordan shifted his weight as if to leave. "Well. All set? Any questions?"

She held up the key to show her new neighbor, and pointed at the offending terra-cotta pot. "I can't believe this! This is *not* good. It's an open invitation for any serial killer to enter your home!"

"Really?"

"Yes! How do I know somebody hasn't made a copy of this?"

He rubbed the back of his neck, looking at her as if *she* was the crazy one. "You can always change the locks, I suppose. If it makes you feel better."

"I mean—why bother to lock your door in the first place, if you just leave the key right next to it in the most obvious spot you can think of?"

Jordan grinned. "Yeah. That's why I never lock my door."

This was a serious culture shock for an L.A. girl.

"And you haven't been murdered in your bed yet?"

"I don't think so, no. Alaska's too cold to be hell and this street is too damn noisy to be heaven." He nodded toward the street. "Last few days before school starts. They are desperate to cram all the fun they can into this weekend. It usually isn't quite this bad."

"That's not a problem for me. I'm a teacher. We're impervious to this kind of noise."

"That must be handy."

"Yup. It's a special course we take at college. 'Closing Your Ears 101.'"

Why was she prattling on like this? Jordan smiled at her stupid joke, and she felt it in her gut. Dammit. But there was no reason to worry—he wasn't even her type. Not even close. Hot, yes, but too scruffy. She liked neat guys. His hair was far too long, unruly and slightly curling, and although he seemed to have shaved recently, it was a bit lopsided, as if he'd been in a hurry.

She liked guys in suits and ties, hair neatly combed until such a time she saw an occasion to change that state. She liked sophisticated aftershave and polished shoes.

This guy's tennis shoes looked like they'd seen better decades.

Feeling better at having reassured herself she would not be the least tempted by her new neighbor, she slid the key in a pocket and stood. She held out a hand. "I guess Jane told you my name, but for a proper introduction—I'm Hailey Rutherford."

"Welcome to Alaska." Jordan took her hand, and as she felt the warmth of it shoot up her arm she thought she detected a flash of interest in his eyes. His hand was large and warm and he held hers for what to her male-ienated mind was a moment too long.

Oh, no.

"I'm married," she blurted out and snatched her hand back, inching her left one behind her back to hide the lack of a ring. "Happily married. Very happily."

Amusement sparkled in his eyes—silver eyes—and a muscle at the corner of his mouth jumped, as if he were holding back a grin. Hailey gritted her teeth as a familiar feeling of folly crept up on her. *Subtlety, girl!*

"Congratulations," Jordan said. "I'm happy for you."

"Daddy!"

One of the little hooligans terrorizing the street came sprinting, taking a running leap up on his father's back.

Dammit. The guy had a family and she'd virtually pointed a stun gun at him without a reason. Her antenna must have rusted.

An elfin face looked at her over his father's shoulder. He looked about seven or eight. He might even be in her class, Hailey realized with excitement. She loved the feeling of meeting a new class, getting to know all the different emerging personalities inside the squirming group of children. "Hi!" the boy said, waving a grubby hand, and Hailey smiled at him.

"Hello. What's your name?"

"Simon. Are you the new Miss Laudin?"

Jordan grabbed his son and put him down. "Her name is *Mrs.* Rutherford. Simon will be in your class," he told Hailey.

"I see!" She smiled broadly at her new pupil. "Nice to meet you, Simon! Maybe you can show me the way to school, then. Ms. Laudin told me it doesn't take more than a couple of minutes to walk there."

The boy stared at her. "I live on the other side of school. Way over there!" He pointed east. "I ride the schoolbus."

"Simon lives with his mother and stepdad," Jordan explained. "But he spends a lot of his time over here with me."

Hailey decided to feel less embarrassed about the stun gun incident. "I see."

"Miss Laudin is a really cool teacher. She's prettier than you, too. And she's a Miss, not a Mrs."

The small pout in the child's face and the petulant

tone had some alarm bells ringing. If the children adored their regular teacher, she might be in for some rough times. It might take a while for them to accept her.

But, well, that was part of the package. Part of the challenge.

"Simon!" Jordan put his hand on his son's shoulder, gently shaking him. "You know very well that was a rude thing to say. Apologize to Mrs. Rutherford."

"Sorry," the boy said, with that unique expression children wore when they were not sorry at all.

"I know you didn't mean to hurt my feelings," she said to the child. "Apology accepted."

The child grunted and ran away again. Hailey dug into her pocket for the rusty key. "Well, I suppose I'll go inside and explore my new home."

"Of course. Will your husband be joining you soon?" Jordan asked.

This was the drawback of spur-of-the-moment decisions. She didn't have a story yet. "No. He's… ah…he's away. We won't be seeing each other again until Christmas."

Jordan nodded. "That's rough. He's away on a job?"

"Yes."

"What sort of a job takes him away so much?"

Questions, questions—and a considerable lack of answers on her part. She peered at him, trying not to notice how well that sweater fit. Could she say it was none of his business?

No. That would be way too rude for the new elementary schoolteacher in such a small town. He was a helpful neighbor, a friend of Jane's. Not good for her image in the neighborhood.

What sort of occupation took husbands away from their wives for months on end? A flash of inspiration struck, and not a moment too soon, judging from the puzzled look dawning on Jordan's face as he waited for an answer. "He works on an oil rig."

"Oil rig? Is that a fact?"

"Yes." Jordan seemed to be waiting for an elaboration, so she elaborated. "You see, he's far away. Siberia. So he can't come home very often."

Jordan raised both eyebrows. "He's in *Siberia?*"

She started praying Siberia had oil rigs. That would teach her to do her homework in good time. "Yes. Siberia. Oil rig."

"Fascinating. I know very little about oil rigs. What kind of work does Mr. Rutherford do?"

Hailey desperately worked at conjuring up a quick image of her fictional husband. Oil rig guy, so her preferred look—a suit and a tie, polished shoes and neatly combed hair—probably wouldn't work. "He's an engineer," she said, hubby's occupation coming to her in a second spark of inspiration. "He maintains their machinery and such." Not bad! She smiled, proud of herself. Excellent save. A vague answer, yet detailed enough not to arouse suspicion. She could do this. Yup. She could lie like a pro.

She could lie like a *man.*

"I see. Well—the house should be okay. If there is a problem, you can talk to me—or call the landlord if it's something serious."

"Serious? Like what?"

Jordan shrugged. "I don't know. I'm just reciting

Jane's message. She left some basic stuff in the fridge. And there are some frozen meals in the freezer.''

"That's great. Very nice of her.''

He nodded. "Jane is a nice person. She told me she'd left plenty of notes around to explain everything—but if you have a problem, my number is on the speed dial.'' He pushed himself away from the fence and grinned at her. He had a killer grin, though of course she wasn't noticing such things either. "But in fact, yelling out the window works just as fine,'' he added as he turned away. "Take care!''

Jane had this guy on speed dial?

And Simon adored Jane.

Hmm. This was interesting.

"Thanks!'' She waved at the little boy hanging on the fence between their houses. "I'll be seeing you in school, Simon!''

The boy frowned, but reluctantly waved back. Hailey grinned, looking forward to seeing the little guy in her class. It was natural for a child to miss a teacher he'd liked, but she'd win him over eventually.

Nowhere—she'd named the house in honor of her parents' complaints about their daughter taking a position out in "nowhere''—was bigger and more elaborate than she had expected; larger than it looked from the outside too. Certainly a lot of room for one person. Jane had left everything very neat and clean—although some surfaces bore a distinct tinge of yellow from all the explanatory sticky notes.

The house seemed sturdy and well-built, and once she had the furnace going, it would no doubt be toasty no matter how cold it got out there. Of course, houses would need to be sturdy to withstand the weather up here in winter.

It was quiet, too, as she'd noticed while waiting outside. Six houses lined the cul-de-sac, each with a large yard. When the children had vanished inside their houses for dinner, it was so quiet she constantly heard the rush of her own blood in her ears. That would go away after a while, of course. She'd get used to the silence, just as she'd before been used to the constant whine of traffic, the pollution in the air and never seeing a clear sky. Then when she got back, she'd have to get acclimatized to L.A. again. It wouldn't be a problem. Homo sapiens was a resilient species. He—*she*—could get used to anything.

Just like she was getting used to being a single woman *not* seeking a man. It had been going great. It *was* going great. She wasn't even looking at men any differently than she looked at the sky or the trees, or that big bag of M&M's on the counter. She wasn't even noticing sexy silver eyes or killer grins or cute—

Nope. She ripped the candy bag open and poured the colorful contents into a glass bowl. She wasn't noticing such things *at all.*

She grabbed a handful of candy and walked toward the back door. The backyard was huge. It vanished into a forest behind the house. She opened the door and stepped out on the porch, taking a deep breath of the fresh, clean air. What would it be like in winter, with a thick blanket of snow on the ground suffocating the branches on the trees, a steely sky above?

Beautiful. Frightening.

Just how bad did winter get up here? her sissy California side whispered.

Well, she'd find out soon enough. It would be an adventure.

There was a hot tub, out on the deck. Interesting. She couldn't quite see herself in there in the midst of winter, with snowflakes falling into the steaming water, but you never knew. It might be fun. Or at any rate, an experience worth trying. She'd never relaxed in a hot water tub with icicles hanging from her hair before.

Adventure, right? her internal California girl asked with a sarcastic twist to her voice. Hailey ignored her. She jumped down off the porch and jogged over the grass toward the low wooden fence and peered over it. Yes. No scrawny decorative trees. It was really a forest. A real forest with real, huge trees. No sissy city trees either.

Just a few steps out of her own backyard and she'd practically be out in the wilderness.

Hailey smiled.

This was so *cool!*

To: All
From: Hailey@MySelfImposedExile.com
Subject: Miss me?
Hi, guys! Guess where I am! No, you'll never guess, so I'll just tell you—ALASKA!

I'm taking part in the teacher exchange program, and before you ask: I didn't tell you because you'd try to talk me out of it. Now it's too late! Don't worry—I'm fine. This is going to be fun.

I'll be here one semester only, so I'll be back before Christmas. Hardly enough time to miss me, but I know you'll try. I'm including my address and phone number—but e-mail is easiest for destitute schoolteachers, isn't it?

Love from up north,
Hailey

The phone rang only a couple of minutes after she'd located Jane's computer and sent an e-mail to all her friends off in cyberspace. As she picked up the phone, Hailey made a mental bet with herself about the identity of the caller.

"You are *where?*"

Yup. Ellen.

Hailey grinned, and in self-defense held the phone several inches away from her ear. She'd done this on purpose—not telling any of her friends what she was up to. They were far too good at talking her out of things. Now, it was too late, but she didn't doubt they'd give it their best shot anyway. Well, they could try all they wanted—it was too late. She had committed to staying here for the next five months. Even if she wanted to, she *couldn't* come back until Christmas. It was perfect.

"Hi, Ellen!"

"Please tell me you were delusional or drunk—or *both*—when you sent that e-mail."

"Sorry to disappoint you."

"Where *are* you?"

"I'm in Alaska," she repeated. "Just like it says in my e-mail."

Ellen cursed. "I was hoping it was one of your stupid practical jokes. What the hell are you doing, moving to *Alaska?* Without even telling me!"

"I'm not *moving*. It's only for one semester."

"What will you be doing there?"

"Same thing as I'm doing at home. Teaching third grade. Their teacher is replacing me back home, you should meet her next week. She's living in my apartment too."

"A total stranger is living in your apartment?"

"Yup. And I'm living in her house. Isn't this teacher exchange program a brilliant idea?"

"*What* teacher exchange program?"

"The new experimental scheme. We all got e-mails about it a few months ago, remember? Opportunity to expand your horizons, seek new challenges, return with new visions, blah blah blah."

"But...but... *Alaska?*" Ellen shrieked. "Hailey, have you lost your marbles?"

"Why? What's wrong with Alaska?"

"There is nothing *wrong* with Alaska—except that it's as far as you can get away from here without emigrating."

"We have phones. E-mail. It's no worse than being a state away.

"You don't know anyone out there!"

"That's the good part. I get away from all the people who have a problem with my decision to stay away from men this year."

"Is *that* what this is about?"

"Partly."

"I see. So your plan is to become a hermit—see the problem?"

"Don't be ridiculous, Ellen! I'm not becoming a hermit!"

"Moving to Alaska where you don't know anybody—without even consulting your closest friends...."

Well, either you're having a nervous breakdown, an early midlife crisis, or you've simply decided on a lifestyle change to go with your new no-men policy and thought a hermit sounded like a nice vocation in life.''

Hailey chose to ignore all jabs about a midlife crisis. The turning-thirty crisis was bad enough. "See? You're part of the worldwide conspiracy! I'm not a hermit just because I'm not dating and decided I needed a change of scenery for a while!''

"Why did you need *Alaskan* scenery?''

"It sounded interesting. A small Alaskan town—something completely different from what I'm used to.''

"Alaska is *cold!*''

"Alaska is beautiful,'' she countered. "The snow, the ice, the northern lights, the landscape...it's gorgeous. I've always wanted to come here. I can't wait for winter to march on.''

"It's *freezing!*''

"It's *fascinating*. You should see the forest behind my house! It's amazing. Looks like something Tarzan could hide in.''

"Tarzan? Now you're talking, if on a different continent. What are Alaskan men like?''

Hailey ignored that. "And I can't wait to see the northern lights!''

"You're a California girl, remember? You'll die of cold!''

"Nah. I'll just need a few more layers of clothes, that's all. It's the most wonderful excuse to buy cashmere!''

"But...but...there are no shopping malls!''

Hailey rolled her eyes. ''Ellen, I'm in Alaska, not at the North Pole. I'm quite close to Anchorage. Of course there are malls.'' She'd just have to hitch a ride there. Or get a car and learn about winter driving.

''Hailey, Alaska is a million miles away!''

She grinned into the phone. ''Exactly.''

Ellen's sigh was eloquent. Hailey could almost visualize her taking her glasses off and pinching the bridge of her nose. ''I don't think you fully understand the gravity of the situation. You're a million miles away!''

''Yes. I heard you the first time. That's the point.''

''Away from *me!*'' Ellen wailed.

''Well, there is that.'' Yes. She would miss her friends. ''But I'll e-mail you. All the time. I'll nag and moan and whine and complain, just like normal. You won't even notice I'm gone.''

''Bah! Why Alaska? There are men in Alaska, you know. There are men everywhere, thank God.''

''I wanted to go to a different environment for a while, get to know different people. Here I won't have my well-intentioned friends to send me on horror dates, no relatives to look at me with sad eyes and talk about marriage and babies—see why this is perfect?''

''You'll make new friends who'll be just as eager to help you find true love. You'll be in the same situation within a month. This does not solve a thing.''

''I'm telling everybody I'm already married. I've already set things in motion.'' A ring. She needed to get a ring. And find a gossipy neighbor to do the job. Jordan didn't seem the type.

''Oh, really? And where's your fictional husband? You keep him up in the attic?''

"This is the brilliant part. He's on an oil rig some-where off the coast of Siberia and is only home for a few weeks every six months."

"Siberia?"

Hailey grimaced. Why did everybody say *Siberia* in that tone of voice? "Yup."

"Why Siberia?"

"I don't know. It was the first thing that came to mind. Oil rig—Siberia. Maybe I saw something about it in one of those Discovery documentaries I watch when I can't sleep."

"Did the documentary show lots of hunky guys on those oil rigs?"

"I don't remember. But now it has one. My husband, Robert."

"Robert?"

"Yes. Robert."

"Are you *nuts?* Would you seriously marry a guy who was on the other side of the world most of the time? What kind of relationship is this anyway?"

"That's not really relevant, is it? He's not real. This is *fiction.*"

Ellen snorted. "Very creative. I need a drink. Does Siberia even have a coast?"

"Of course it does! It's huge. It has to have a coast."

"A real coast, or just a frozen chunk of ice?"

There was an awkward silence filled with mutual embarrassment over their geographical shortcomings. "Sure it has a coast," Hailey said uncertainly. "I mean, of course it doesn't have sunny beaches, but it has to have a coast!"

"A husband in Siberia. How convenient. He'll be

right next door. All you have to do is cross the North Pole. But let's get back to the important issue. *Me.*''

Hailey chuckled. "I'm going to miss you too, Ellen.''

"Who's going to watch black-and-white movies with me Sunday evenings? Huh?''

They went a few more rounds before Hailey hung up, breathing a sigh of relief. Everybody would know soon, even those she hadn't e-mailed.

CNN had nothing on Ellen when it came to broadcasting news.

The sticky notes were all over the house, everything from explaining eccentricities of the dishwasher to a motherly reminder to wear sunscreen in the winter sun. Hailey gathered them together as she came across them, smiling as a mental picture of Jane came together in her mind. She knew Jane was about her age, but with all the maternal advice littering the house she couldn't help but picture a gray bun and pince-nez glasses. Maybe her suspicions about Jane and Jordan were way off base.

She plucked a note off the kitchen faucet and stuck it under a refrigerator magnet with a bunch of other kitchen messages. She'd probably be coming across additional ones for weeks to come.

The phone rang again, only minutes after she'd finished unpacking and was in the process of choosing a yellow note—marked frozen dinner to zap.

"Okay, you've had two hours. Ready to come home now?'' Ellen asked without preamble.

Hailey laughed. "No.''

"Do you know the male to female ratio up in Alaska?"

"Um...no."

"I just looked it up for you. It's not in your favor. You're much better off back here where there aren't enough men to go around."

"There may be more men here, but I'm not available here, and there is no one to contradict me on that. This is perfect."

Ellen snorted. "This isn't going to work. You must know, Hailey, that if you swear off men, you're going to have Mr. Rights lining up on your doorstep. It's a cosmic law."

"Cosmic laws are meant to be broken."

"Just remember, don't walk away from true love if it comes knocking."

"True love again?"

"I'm serious. Principles aren't worth such a sacrifice. If the right guy comes knocking—don't send him away without a test drive. Promise?"

There was a sound at the door. Hailey raised an eyebrow, for a second wondering if Ellen could have staged this. "Hold on, I think True Love may be knocking on my door right now."

"I'll hold," Ellen replied, but Hailey took the cordless phone with her. She checked the peephole, but didn't see anything. She opened the door, irritated to notice the lack of a security chain.

"Meow," said someone politely, and she lowered her gaze to meet a green gaze from about ankle level. It was a tiny kitten, adorable with its narrow orange and white stripes. It squeezed through the opening and bolted into the house. Hailey peered around outside, but saw no one, so she closed the door again.

"Well, we seem to have True Love," she told Ellen. "A kitten just came asking for asylum and I have no idea where it went."

Ellen oohed. "Great. Boy or girl? Is it a stray looking for a home? I hear they make great self-cleaning litter boxes these days."

"I can't keep it," Hailey protested, walking from room to room looking for the cat. "I don't know anything about animals. And I can't take it with me when I go back home. Pets aren't allowed at my apartment."

"Don't panic. You probably won't be able to keep it anyway. Most likely it's a neighbor's cat."

Hailey squeezed the phone between ear and shoulder and dove after a swinging tail into a kitchen cupboard. "Out of there, you little thief," she muttered. "How can you smell the tuna inside the can? And how did you manage to open the cupboard?"

"The cat opened a cupboard?"

"Well, I didn't leave it open, and now he's inside." Hailey grabbed hold of the cat by the middle and pulled it out of the cupboard. A small tail flicked in anger, and then the kitten hissed at her.

"It's a he?"

"I don't know." She held the cat up and tried to check out the relevant body parts. "I have no idea. Is there an easy way to tell?"

"Hmm. Pink or blue collar? Or a name tag?"

"No collar. Hold on—someone's knocking again." She flung the door open, phone cradled between her ear and shoulder, cat digging its claws into her other shoulder. This time, there was a human on her doorstep. A hot, scruffy one.

Of course it would be *his* cat.

"Hi again. Did you get a feline visitor recently?" Hailey shifted, and Jordan caught a look at the cat hanging from her shoulder. "I see you two have met."

"This your cat?" Hailey tried to remove the kitten, but the claws were stuck to her sweater—and a few embedded in her skin. "Ouch! Is it a boy or a girl?"

"Female."

"Are you sure? She's behaving an awful lot like a boy."

"I'm a vet, I should know. She's female."

"And she's yours?"

"No, she's not my cat. That's Helena. And she seems to be stuck to you. Can I help?"

Helena meowed, digging her claws in deeper. Hailey yelped. "Yikes! What's she trying to do, give me a paw-shaped tattoo? Get her off me!"

"I'm trying." Jordan leaned closer as he dug Helena's claws one by one out of Hailey's shoulder. After a small eternity he finally straightened up with the tiny kitten in his arms. Hailey noticed she didn't dig into *his* skin with her lethal little claws.

Instead she was purring.

Typical female.

"You okay?" Jordan asked.

"Huh?" Much like Helena, she'd gotten distracted. It was the way he smelled. No sophisticated cologne, of course, it wouldn't go with the rest of him—but something even better. Outdoorsy scent. Natural and fresh. Primitive. Masculine. Undeniably sexy.

Okay, Hailey, for that thought you spend an extra half hour on the treadmill.

Dammit! This wasn't boding well.

"Yeah, I'm fine. I think." She rubbed her shoulder. "No lasting damage. She's so cute! Orange cats are so cute. Does she live nearby?"

"She's nobody's cat. She showed up a couple of weeks ago and begs food from everybody in the street." He stroked the kitten and she meowed on top of her purr, butting his palm with her tiny head. "She's used to hanging out with Jane, so you'll probably be seeing a lot of her." He put the cat down on the doorstep, and she sped back inside, with only a short pause to rub against Hailey's legs, leaving another fine layer of soft orange hair.

"She found a can of tuna in the kitchen. A whole pile of cans in fact. She seemed to know the way."

His lips quirked. "That would explain her love for Jane. And her sudden love for you." His shoulders lifted in a shrug, drawing her unwilling attention to some excellent hidden physique under that sweater, and then he started to turn away. "Anyway, I just wanted to tell you about her, since I saw her heading your way."

Hailey looked back. The cat was prancing back and forth by the kitchen cabinet, impatiently waiting for her to come and dish out the tuna. "What do I do with her?" she called after Jordan.

He turned back, shrugging again, his hands in the pockets of his worn—but damn well-fitting—jeans. "She's a house-squatting stray. Let her stay if you like, else just show her the door. She'll get the picture if you don't feed or pet her, and find another prey."

"Throw her outside?" That seemed a bit cruel. "Where will she sleep?"

Jordan chuckled as he jumped over the fence. "Anywhere," he called back. "She's a *cat*. Cats know better than anyone that there's a sucker born every minute."

Hailey shut the door and leaned against it, eyes closed. No, no, no, no.

Why did a guy like that have to live next door? Why did she have to feel drawn to the first man she met up here? Was it her addiction, already pushing her toward the first available man?

Well, she would damn well fight it. She could, and she would.

She'd completely forgotten about Ellen when there was a sound from the phone, still clenched in her hand. She brought it to her ear. "Hi. Sorry to leave you hanging."

"I didn't mind. I heard the entire thing. Who was that?"

Hailey gritted her teeth to keep her voice steady. Nonchalant but not too nonchalant, or Ellen would catch on. Ellen was far too good at reading voices, faces—thoughts, even. "Nobody. Just a neighbor. Someone Jane sent over to give me the key."

Ellen's voice turned smug. "For a nobody, he sounds pretty sexy."

Right. Utter failure. What had she expected? "Nope. Not sexy at all. He's sixty-nine, bald, toothless and absolutely not my type."

"You're lying. He sounds hunky. All that low timbre... Mmm. Oh, yes, I like him."

"It's just a voice! We all have one!"

"I bet he could give you goose bumps if he were to whisper something sweet into your ear. Like, say, on a dance floor? Holding you close, your head resting on his shoulder breathing in his masculine scent as you softly sway together to a romantic ballad, your bodies in perfect synchrony…"

"Oh, for crying out loud, Ellen! Shut up! Go write a poem!"

"In a minute. I just need a few vital statistics, then I'll stop, promise. What's his name?"

It was easier to give in and get it over with. "His name is Jordan Halifax. He's a vet. Probably around thirty-five or something. He has a kid in my class. That enough info for you?"

"A kid? But he's single?"

"Yes."

"Most excellent. What does he look like?"

"Gray eyes, thick, wavy brown hair, sort of scruffy look but he makes it work. Tall, wears jeans and sweaters in that way that could make women in their weaker moments want to rip them off. Happy?"

"Wow! You've really *looked* at him, haven't you? You only met him a couple of hours ago!"

"I know," Hailey confessed, feeling miserable. "He's just that kind of a guy. You should come visit and check him out for yourself. He's not for me. I already told him I'm married, okay? I made it perfectly clear I'm off limits."

Ellen sighed so loudly that Hailey almost expected a gust of wind to blow through the phone. "I knew it. Didn't I tell you so? A potential Mr. Right shows up your first day in Alaska, and you kick him out."

"Goodbye, Ellen!"

*　　*　　*

That evening, Hailey discovered she was indeed a sucker for cats. She opened a can of tuna for the little creature, then allowed her to crawl into her lap and spend the evening there, purring. She could hardly bear to disturb the kitten when it was time to go to bed, but Helena curled up on a sofa cushion and seemed to be happy. Just in case, Hailey made a nest out of a fleece blanket and deposited her there.

She walked upstairs to the bedroom and crawled into bed, but it was hard to get to sleep when dusk never showed up. Close to midnight Hailey found herself wide awake, staring out the window at the eerie light. Not night, not day.

It was almost magic.

Combined with the day's events, it was also a sure-fire recipe for insomnia.

CHAPTER TWO

AFTER six weeks, Hailey had gotten used to the climate growing slowly colder, and she'd fallen in love with her class of eight-year-olds.

But she had to admit she was getting a bit lonely.

She missed her friends—and because of her fictional husband she was nervous about making new friends. Her lie was so flimsy that anyone who got close to her would see through it immediately. She'd already frowned in confusion several times on being referred to as "Mrs."—and had to explain it away as being relatively newly married.

Yeah, right. And her brand new husband on the other side of the world. As if she'd ever let a hypothetical husband get away with *that*. Ha!

Some things were easier up here, despite temptation living next door. She'd given it a lot of thought, and had to confess to herself that annoyance with her friends' interference wasn't the only thing that had caused her to flee. She'd been too close to giving up—too close to finding it pointless to keep to her resolution. Maybe it was pointless—but even so, it was worth a try.

She was happy with her decision. This was good for her. There was freedom in being unavailable, freedom in spending Saturday evening curled up with a book and a purring cat. Not that she'd said her final goodbye to parties and clubs for ever and ever—but this was also life. Singledom wasn't going anywhere. It would be waiting for her in January. She'd probably be a bit rusty, but she was sure she'd have a new outlook on life and love, a *healthy* outlook.

The small school turned out to be a fun workplace. Most of her colleagues were quite a bit older than she was, but there was good morale. Her class was small and the kids were great—once they were over the disappointment of Jane being away for the semester. Even Simon came around, the suspicious look slowly vanishing off his face, and she suspected she had little Helena to thank for that. The two of them spent a lot of time playing in her backyard during Simon's weekends with his dad and some of Helena's charm seemed to rub off on Hailey, especially when she started offering Simon milk and cookies to go along with Helena's milk and tuna.

"Sure you don't mind him coming over?" Jordan asked, leaning on the fence between their yards. His boy was halfway up a tree—the cat was even higher.

"No," she told him for the umpteenth time. She enjoyed their neighborly chats over the fence. Somehow, it felt safe with the fence between them and his child playing close by. "Don't worry about it, it's fine. Helena has an endless source of energy and I don't. If she runs around with Simon a bit, maybe she'll let me sleep tonight." Hailey grimaced. "She likes to hunt my toes at four in the morning."

Helena had taken up double residence of her house and Jordan's. She seemed to like the freedom of two homes to go to, which sometimes resulted in a double dinner. She always spent the nights at Hailey's house—Hailey suspected Jordan didn't let her sleep in his bed.

Simon came running, once again complaining Helena had climbed a tree too far for him to reach her.

"She'll come down," Hailey told him. "Doesn't she always? She's just teasing you. She'll be down as soon as you turn your back and pretend you're not even looking for her."

Simon's dark hair and silver eyes were a lot like his father's—but he got his delicate facial features from his mother. Hailey had met her on Open Night and immediately noticed the resemblance.

"Mrs. Rutherford, why don't you wear a wedding ring?" Simon asked, squinting up at her against the sun. "Aren't you supposed to, you know, so everybody knows you can't be their girlfriend?"

That probably *was* one purpose of wedding rings. And a good idea it was. Hailey stared at her ringless hand, searching for an answer. "Well…"

"Mick says his Mom says maybe you don't like your husband anymore."

"Simon! You know better than that. Apologize to your teacher."

"No, it's okay—it's a natural question, I suppose." Dammit. She'd never gotten around to getting a ring— and then she'd forgotten. She hadn't imagined the eight-year-olds would gossip about it. She flexed her fingers and smiled at Simon. "My hands have swelled since I've been up here," she lied. "My ring doesn't fit anymore. It's probably the climate changes."

"So you still like your husband?"

"Uh, yes. I still like him. It's just my fingers are so swollen…"

"No need to explain." Jordan's grin was enigmatic, but the frown aimed at his son was clear-cut. "That's enough, Simon. Don't be rude."

She looked at him sideways, trying to decipher the look on his face. Did he suspect she was lying? It was impossible to tell from the bland look in his eyes.

"When does it start to snow?" Simon whined, staring up at the sky. His father rolled his eyes.

"Simon, do you honestly think we don't get enough snow around here? Remember last year? We thought spring would never arrive."

"I can't wait for the snow! I want to go sledding, and skiing and ice skating…"

Jordan grinned at Hailey, a wry grin from one suffering snow-shoveling, ice-scraping adult to another, she supposed, but of course she'd never shoveled snow in her life. She was sort of looking forward to the experience, but if she said anything about that, it would probably have two identical jaws drop. One smooth—the other a bit bristly. How come she was *now* finding that sort of thing attractive? Must be something in the air.

"There will be time enough to play in the snow, Simon," Jordan told his son. "I promise."

"Maybe I've forgotten how to ski," Simon complained, and his father ruffled his hair.

"Then you'll have fun learning it again."

Simon tore off again.

"Is he behaving in school?" Jordan asked. "He's got so much energy…"

"Yeah, he's fine." *Right,* she reminded herself and stood up straight, folding her arms on her chest. This was her student's father. It wasn't professional to stare at his lips and wonder if he was a good kisser. "He's not the quietest one in my class, I'll admit, but he's a good kid. Very bright and inquisitive, too."

"Yes." Jordan stared after his son, wistfulness in his face. "I wish I had more time with him. There's so much of his life that I miss. Sometimes I don't see him for as long as two weeks and it actually seems he's grown since I last saw him."

She made a sound of sympathy. "I know. That's what happens with so many kids after a divorce. It's inevitable, I suppose."

"We're not divorced," Jordan said. "I was never married to his mother."

"Oh." She shook her head. "Sorry. He bears your name and everything—I just assumed."

"Of course. Glad to hear you didn't know. That must mean Simon isn't teased about it in school."

"Not at all—well, not that I'm aware of. Of course, teachers don't see everything, but I don't think anybody's teased about being illegit…ah…well, nobody's teased about things like that anymore. And his mother and stepfather came to Open Night, so he had two parents there…" She trailed off at the look on Jordan's face. "Oops."

Jordan swore under his breath. "Don't get me wrong—I think it's wonderful he has a good step-father…. And I want them to be a complete family…. I try not to complain about it but sometimes it really feels like they're trying to exclude me. It's 'better' that I don't attend this and that, it would just be confusing to Simon…"

"Nobody can replace you in Simon's life."

"His stepfather has been raising him since he was four years old."

"You're his *father*. Anyone can see he adores you! You should come to school functions too. A lot of kids have three or four parents there. If there's anything today's kids know all about, it's the complexities of the post-nuclear family."

"Post-nuclear family?"

"It's a genuine scientific term," she said defensively.

"If it's anything like post-modernism, I don't like it."

She peered at him. He was joking. Right? Sometimes it was hard to tell if he was joking or not. She wasn't used to interpreting these kinds of dry ironic remarks. "Well—post-nuclear is as good a description as any, I guess," she said. "And you're doing fine as a post-nuclear father. Don't worry about Simon. He'll be fine."

Jordan chuckled. "Thanks for defending me, Hailey. His mother seems to think my dogs and the other animals are more an attraction for Simon than I am."

Hailey pictured the petite dark-haired lady she'd met at school. She'd seemed *nice*. This was *not* nice. "She said that to you?"

"It sort of slipped out, she didn't mean to be cruel." He shrugged. "We have an okay relationship, no fights—but it's obvious she wishes her husband was Simon's father instead of me."

"Has it been long since you two broke up?"

"Yeah. Cynthia didn't realize she was pregnant until she was four months along. We'd split up a couple

of months before.'' He shrugged again. ''She didn't
think there was any point in trying to work things out
just for the sake of the child, and in retrospect she was
probably right.''

''Don't let her push you away from your son. Don't
let anybody do that.''

''No. I won't.''

They were silent for a while, watching the child and
the cat play. Both of them came running, as they did
every few minutes, and this time Simon climbed up
on the fence and boasted, ''Daddy is coming to school
next week!''

''Right, I heard something about that. You talk to
the kids about animals. That's already next week?''

''Yeah. It's been going on for several years. The
kids also visit my clinic once a year, in small groups.''

Next week! She'd thought she had more time. She
wasn't at all sure how she felt about Jordan invading
her safe, neutral school environment. While she kept
him on the other side of the fence—literally—things
had been going fine. She really didn't need him to
invade her thoughts at work. ''I see. Sounds like…''
She had been about to say *fun,* but as Simon had wandered off again she changed it to reflect her true feelings. ''Sounds like utter chaos! How do the animals
react? They're sick to begin with, aren't they?''

''I wouldn't do this if it traumatized or hurt the
animals.'' He seemed almost offended. ''Only two or
three kids go in at a time, and they receive a stern
lecture beforehand on the dos and don'ts. We never
have any problems. The kids know the consequence—
no visit next year if they misbehave.''

She chuckled. ''I suspect you're responsible for

about half my class wanting to be vets when they grow up.''

''Children and animals have a special affinity. It's beautiful to watch.''

They watched Simon inch out on a precarious branch and Helena jump nimbly down, just as he was about to reach for her. Simon wailed in frustration as he watched the cat saunter away with her tail held high. Jordan chuckled. ''See? Special affinity. She knows exactly how to drive that boy crazy.''

Late-night phone calls from drunken exes really should be a legitimate reason for calling in sick.

What a night.

Hailey trudged into the school Monday morning feeling disoriented and fuzzy. A combination of sleep deprivation and the pitch-black Alaska mornings did that to you. She said a quick hello to the other teachers, then went straight to her classroom, hoping she didn't seem too rude. She just wasn't in the mood— or the state—to talk to anyone. Calling in sick had been tempting—but hanging around the house all day, brooding, probably wasn't smart either.

She'd just have to soldier on.

''Why are your eyes so red?'' A little girl was staring up at her, wide-eyed and worried. ''Did you hurt yourself?''

Did I? Hailey asked herself. She felt drained. Crying was tiring. Sobbing this hard for an entire night was exhausting, and her eyes—her whole face—were still stinging. She'd probably have to hang her pillow out to dry.

"I'm fine, Alison," she told the child, "It's just my makeup. Don't worry."

The child's eyes widened even more. "Makeup makes you look like you've been crying?"

"No…" Saved by the bell. She shooed Alison off to her seat and started the day, ignoring the curious stares of the children. She didn't have a better explanation for them—if she tried, it would just confuse them even further.

Lesson learned: no crying on school nights!

The day passed with agonizing slowness. Fortunately it was a short one—around noon the kids all gathered in the gym for Jordan's show-and-tell, a precursor to the individual visits to the clinic, which would start next week. She was impressed with his performance. In her experience, so many visitors to schools had no idea of how to talk to children.

She stayed away from Jordan—not difficult considering how the kids crowded around him. She didn't need more people to notice the puffiness around her eyes.

"Hi." That evening, just as she was about to zap another tasteless meal, Jordan was standing on her doorstep, smiling but looking rather awkward. She smiled back.

"Hi."

There was silence. He seemed to be trying to figure out how to say something, but without much luck. Had he come to talk about Simon? She leaned against the door post and raised an eyebrow. "What's up? Did you come to borrow a cup of sugar or something?"

"What? Yes. Sugar."

"You're here to borrow sugar?"

"No." He shook his head. "Sorry. I just wanted to check on you... I talked to Simon on the phone just now, and he told me you'd been crying in school today. Is there something I can do?"

Little gossips. Were all the kids telling their parents their teacher had suffered a nervous breakdown in class? She shook her head. "I wasn't crying in school. My eyes were a bit puffy this morning. The children were curious, but it's nothing at all. Allergy, maybe. I'm fine." She grimaced. "Too bad if the kids misunderstood."

Jordan frowned. "Allergy? Do you think you may be allergic to the cat?"

"No!" she hastened to say. She'd fallen in love with the cat and nobody would be taking Helena away from her. Well, not until it was time to leave—and when that day came, she was sure she'd miss the cat more than she'd missed any of her ex-boyfriends. "No allergy. I may be coming down with a mild cold or something, nothing more serious. It's nothing, really."

He nodded. "Okay. So it's not like...I mean, Bobby is fine and everything?"

"Bobby?" Her mind went blank. She mentally tallied off the kids in her class. No Bobby. No Robert. "Bobby?" she repeated, cautiously. A kid in the street? One of her fellow teachers? No. Jordan was staring at her frowning, and the pressure mounted. She should know this. "Bobby is..." Could it be one of the school's guinea pigs Jordan had seen this afternoon? One of them had been sick. "Was Bobby the guinea pig who kept sneezing?"

"I'm talking about Bobby Rutherford," Jordan clarified, skepticism emanating from him. "Your husband, remember?"

Uh, oh. "Right!" She laughed, too heartily. "Of course. I didn't know who you were referring to there for a minute. *Robby!*"

"I was sure you'd called him Bobby."

"His friends call him Bobby. I call him Robby. I like to be different. I never think of him as Bobby."

"I see." He shifted and Hailey looked over his shoulder. She didn't want to see the look on his face. He was probably grinning. Did he know? Did he suspect? Or—her last hope—did he just think she was hopelessly scatterbrained? "Anyway—when Simon said you'd been crying I thought I'd check on you. Thought maybe something had happened to your husband. Oil rigs are dangerous workplaces..."

"It's very nice of you, but I'm fine. I'm perfect." She shook her head. "I can't believe everybody's going nuts because of puffy eyes!"

"Never lived in a small town before, have you?"

"No."

He grinned. "We worry."

"Is this going to be in the weekly newspaper?"

"It might." She gasped, and he laughed. "I'm just kidding."

"Phew!"

"Well—take care."

"So you won't be needing that sugar after all?"

He chuckled. "No."

She closed the door and leaned against it, biting her lip and clenching her eyes shut. Close call. Nice save, though. But keeping up a lie could be terribly complicated. There were all sorts of side effects she hadn't anticipated.

Well. It was just for a few months more. She'd live.

She grabbed her laptop, plugged in the modem and fell onto the sofa. She needed Ellen right now, needed to tell her all about last night's horrible phone call, but face-to-face girl-talk was out. She'd have to make do with e-mail.

To: Ellen
From: Hailey@MySelfImposedExile.com
Subject: I miss you!
Yes, I do, dammit. And I have a reason too. You'll never guess what happened yesterday. After all this time, Dan actually had the nerve to call me, wanting to get back together! Oh, God.

I really needed you to be there and hold my hand while I told him where to go and what to do. It wasn't pretty, but I did it. Who gave him my number? You know everybody. Find out for me, and I'll put that person's head on a stake.

I spent the whole night crying—and I'm not even sure why. It's not like I want him back, and there's even this tiny gloating part of me, jumping up and down because he tried to come crawling back, but still—I was up all night, bawling. I was so distracted I almost blew my cover to the neighbor. I think I'm okay, though. He probably has me down as an airhead blonde, but hey, as long as everybody thinks I'm a *married* airhead blonde…

Why is life so confusing?

Love,
Red-eyed Hailey

"Are you okay?"

Hailey laughed and curled up on the sofa with the phone pressed to her ear. Ellen's voice brought her back home in seconds. "Hi! I just pressed the Send key five seconds ago."

"I don't know where he got your phone number. Jerk. Had he been drinking?"

"Probably. Don't think he would have called me sober." She cackled, feeling better already. Writing the e-mail had caused the tears to start gushing again, but just the sound of Ellen's indignant voice cheered her up. "Boy, he must have been sorry this morning."

"Serves him right. So, tell me. What did he say? What did you say? Will he call again?"

Hailey grimaced and felt her throat tighten. "He said he loved me. That was the worst part."

"He did? *Dan* used the word *love?*"

"Yup. *Now* he tells me. Too little, too late." It had been months. Months of development and growth—she wasn't even the same person anymore. Had last night been grief over a past relationship—or her past self?

"Why now?"

"It was his birthday. I didn't even remember."

"That's great! Good for you."

"Yeah. But apparently he got all mushy about turning thirty-five. Apparently he has now decided that not only does he want commitment, he wants marriage and children, too."

"Ah. Early midlife crisis. Oh, God. And? What did you say?"

"I said it was over and I wasn't interested, ever. Then I said goodbye, happy birthday, and put the phone down."

"That was it?"

"He called again. I picked up, said I'd leave the phone off the hook and then change my number if he called again. He didn't."

Ellen drew in a sharp breath of admiration—or shock. Hailey wasn't sure. "You're *tough!* I'm proud of you!"

Hailey snorted. "Right. Then I went to bed—at six o'clock—and started crying. Only paused for the occasional glass of water when my fluid level became dangerously low."

"He's not worth the tears. Especially not now. You're over him, right? He's not worth your tears."

"No." Hailey tilted her head back, staring up toward the ceiling. She'd made some discoveries during the night. "He's not worth it. But *I* am. That's the problem."

Ellen sighed, then gave a distressed cry. "You need me! We need a girls' night with pizzas and popcorn and black-and-white movies and lots of tissues while we lecture each other on the meaning of life. *Now* do you see why moving to Alaska wasn't a good idea?"

Hailey felt a tear sneak up on her—this one sentimental. She tried not to sniff and give it away, but failed utterly. "Ellen, I *do* miss you."

"Are you crying again?"

"Nah. Only good tears. Only 'I'm so lucky I have good friends' tears."

"Are you going to be okay?"

She smiled. "Yes. I'm going to be just fine."

"Seen Mr. Sexy-Voice recently?"

"Ellen!"

"Hey, it's one of the Ten Commandments. Love thy neighbor."

"Well, I…"

"Or was it Love thy neighbor's ass? I forget."

"Ellen!"

"Just checking how pious you're being."

"You're impossible, do you know that?"

"I just want you to live happily ever after. If a rugged Alaskan prince is what it takes, then so be it."

"Let's talk about *your* love-life for a change."

"No news on that front. Now, your Jane on the other hand…"

"Jane?"

"She and our vice principal are getting along awfully well."

"But Jane is…"

"Jane is what? Please don't tell me she has a husband and kids waiting for her at home."

"No. No—nothing like that. I just got the impression…" Hailey cursed, relieved, and at the same time annoyed at herself for being relieved. "Never mind."

"You know better than to say 'never mind' to me."

"I thought perhaps she and Jordan might have something going. I've nothing to back it up though. It's just a feeling."

"You mean, wishful thinking."

"No…"

"You *want* that guy to be off limits, don't you?"

"He is."

"Well, judging by the way Jane was draped all over Mr. Hollis in the parking lot after the teacher's conference last week, Jordan and Jane are definitely not involved."

"I see. And what about you? Seeing anyone interesting?"

"Nope. Periscope actively sweeping the area, but no Mr. Right sightings."

"Well, keep up the search, Ensign."

"You've got it, Commander."

CHAPTER THREE

IT STARTED to snow early in October. Hailey could hardly believe it when she woke up to find a strange kind of brightness hammering in through the windows—but snow covered the ground and wafted down from silvery cloud-covered skies. She opened the window wide and breathed in the fresh air. It was almost fragrant.

Fortunately, her pragmatic side noted, it was only a couple of inches. Enough for the kids to play with, but so little snow couldn't turn out to be a problem for the adults, could it?

Wrong, she soon learned, as she walked past a long line of backed-up commuters on her way to work. Many classes started late because the teacher was stuck in traffic somewhere, and there was a lot of cursing going on in the teachers' lounge.

It snowed all day, and by the middle of the day a couple of inches had morphed into almost a foot. The kids were ecstatic. Obviously even Alaskan kids were excited at the first sign of snow, and she played with them during the breaks, building snowmen, fortresses and having snowball fights. She was just as disappointed as the kids were when the bell summoned them back inside.

"I've hardly ever seen snow before," she explained to her fellow teachers as she tried to hang her wet coat somewhere far away from their dry ones. "It's incredible, isn't it? It's like the world has turned into one big, giant Christmas card. I love it!''

"Just wait until you've been here a few more months,'' the vice principal grumbled. "You'll be cursing the snow with the rest of us. Thank God the weekend is coming up.''

Mrs. Crumbs gave him the evil eye. She tended to do that whenever he mentioned weekends or family time in front of Hailey. Mrs. Crumbs seemed to think weekends were hell for Hailey, all by herself with a faraway husband.

"Have you heard from your husband lately, dear?'' she asked gently, and Hailey felt a familiar stab of guilt.

"Oh, yes, we talk on the phone all the time,'' she said brightly, trying to conjure up an image of her husband. Robby—Bobby to his friends, but not to her. *Robby*. "And e-mail, too. We write lots and lots of e-mail.''

"Better save those,'' Mrs. Crumbs sighed. "I don't think printouts wrapped in a ribbon can possibly equal handwritten love letters, but I suppose they have to be the modern day equivalent. As long as he *is* writing love letters…''

"Of course he is.'' Yup. That's just the kind of thing Robby would do. Robby was loving, faithful, fun, dependable, loyal, sexy and intelligent. He had expressive eyes with long lashes that didn't take anything away from his masculinity. He was tall but not too tall, muscular but not too bulky, did the dishes without being asked and only had a moderate obsession with baseball. She was very close to falling in love with her own creation.

Unfortunately, Robby bore an eerie resemblance to Jordan, a fact that had escaped Hailey's conscious notice until it was too late and his image firmly etched in her mind—and the description she'd given Mrs. Crumbs. She'd literally had to mop the sweat off her brow after a particularly intense interrogation about why she didn't carry her husband's picture in her purse.

Lying was much harder than it looked.

"Robby is doing fine," she answered with a smile. "Of course we miss each other, but well—that can't be helped. And we're used to it by now. The reunions are that much sweeter for it."

"Of course...when you have children..." Mrs. Crumbs let the sentence trail off, but stared at her with head tilted to the side and eyebrows raised in a tentative question. Hailey frowned. What would Robby do if they had a baby? Would he give up his job to stay home with her and the little one?

Of course he would. A man like Robby would want to see his child grow up. He wouldn't want to be on the other side of the world six months at a time. He wouldn't even consider it, not even if she bravely ordered him not to give up a job he loved for the sake of her or the little one with his silver eyes and her blond hair...

She noticed Mrs. Crumbs was staring at her a bit differently, at the same time she realized she'd been staring into distance, hand protectively splayed across her stomach. She snatched it away and folded her hands together to keep them out of mischief. *Idiot. Get a grip, Hailey! You're not inventing a pregnancy to go with the fictional husband!* "Oh, I expect he'll want to give up his job then," she said with a smile. "Robby wouldn't want to miss seeing his children grow up. He loves kids."

"He sounds like such a fine man," Mrs. Crumbs sighed wistfully. "How did the two of you meet? If you don't mind my asking, of course…"

"Through friends," she said vaguely, very tempted to make up a romantic story of a first encounter at the beach under the stars, or eyes meeting across a crowded room. Maybe it was time to try her hand at writing fiction. Her imagination was certainly getting a workout. "You know, we moved in similar circles."

Mrs. Crumbs had moved closer, her warm blue eyes wide open in interest. She was close to retirement and had lost her own husband several years ago, but her belief in romance was still going strong.

"So it wasn't love at first sight?"

"Oh, yes, it was," Hailey assured her. Of course it had been love at first sight. With a man like Robby, how could it not be? "It just took me a while to realize it… I'd been burned before, you see, and wasn't really looking for a man. In fact, I wanted to avoid men for a while, but Robby was so…. Well, he was special."

"He sure is," Mrs. Crumbs agreed. "I can tell just from hearing you talk about him. You two have something unique."

Hailey bit her lip, guilt gnawing at her insides. Would lying to the sweetest old lady in the world send her to purgatory?

To: Ellen
From: Hailey@MySelfImposedExile.com
You're not going to believe this. My roof is leaking!

Remember how I talked about fixing my own roof—well, it looks like I'll have to do just that. It's been snowing like mad for the past couple of days, and I guess the warmth from within makes the snow on top of my roof melt…and guess where it all goes! Yes! I was awakened at five o'clock this morning—a Saturday!—by Chinese water torture.

I've called the landlord, and he's sending someone, but not until the snow lets up. So—I'm climbing up on my roof with my new tools—yes, tools!—to see what I can do. I love it! This is what independence is all about! I'm not entirely sure I'll be able to fix anything, but it's worth a try.

I'll tell you all about it in my next e-mail.

On top of the world—or at least on top of the roof very soon,

Hailey

The weather had really started playing up on Friday evening, and after one look out the window Saturday morning Jordan decided to spend the weekend indoors. His two dogs, however, did not agree, and he was forced to take them outside in the snowstorm. "Just a short walk, guys," he warned them as he opened the door and strode into the thigh-high drifts. "Very short."

Sam and Daisy immediately ran toward Hailey's house, but he called them back. She'd seemed rather nervous of the dogs, and probably wouldn't welcome their enthusiastic barking at her door. He glanced at her house—he'd found himself doing that a lot the past couple of months—and did a double take.

It was no mirage. Hailey was up on the roof, kneeling near the chimney, wearing a pink and green snowsuit.

"What the hell are you doing up there?" he shouted, kicking himself when she twisted around, startled. Stupid, to shout like that. She could have fallen. Not that falling off the roof would be all that dangerous with so much snow to break her fall, but still, she was out of her element here and he should have been more careful.

"My roof is leaking," she yelled back. "It looks like it needs big repairs, but for now I just want to fix the biggest leak in my bedroom."

Jordan bit back a swearword. The snowstorm aside—had that woman ever heard of hypothermia? Frostbite? The risks of unpredictable weather conditions? He shooed the dogs into his backyard and jumped the fence into Hailey's, circling the house until he located the ladder she'd used to get up there. Already the rungs were heavy with snow, slippery with ice—that crazy woman could break her neck just getting down if she wasn't careful. Hell, falling off the roof was probably safer. He scaled the ladder as quickly as he could, and pulled himself up on the roof.

City girl. She'd probably kill herself out here if she didn't get herself a baby-sitter. And for now, it looked like he was stuck with the job. Carefully he made his way across the roof to where she was kneeling, trying to work a screwdriver under a shingle, a hammer clenched in her other hand. It was pretty obvious she had no idea what she was doing, but he had to give her an A for effort. "Get down off the roof and go inside, Hailey. I'll see what I can do."

She yanked her hammer away as he reached out to take it from her. "No!"

No? What did she mean, no? *"No?"*

"No, *thank you,*" she amended, like he'd been criticizing her manners. "I'm fine. I don't need your help just because I'm a woman, so knock off the machismo. It doesn't impress me."

He looked at her. She was shivering inside her flimsy snowsuit, hands clenched around the sissy-looking hammer and screwdriver. Her tools looked like something designed for Barbie, but her scowl was a more formidable weapon.

"Do you know what you're doing?"

"No," she confessed reluctantly, almost pouting. "But you only learn by doing."

"Do you seriously think this is the time and place to learn the basics of roof repair?"

"Well, my roof is leaking—which would make this an excellent time to learn about roof repair, yes."

"I recommend a nice session with a DIY book first. Inside, in front of the fire with hot chocolate and marshmallows."

"You are *so* patronizing. Go down and drink the cocoa yourself. I'm finishing this."

He looked at her handiwork. He wasn't sure, but it seemed like she'd intended to cover the hole with several layers of plastic shopping bags. Inventive for a temporary solution, but probably not very useful. "What exactly is it you're trying to do?"

"I'll tell you tomorrow."

"Why not now?"

"Because you're going to tell me it's all wrong and it won't work."

"If that were true, wouldn't you want to know?"

"Yes. Tomorrow."

She took stubborn to a new level. He had to admire her guts, even though it was extremely frustrating that she wouldn't allow him to help. He had to fight to stop himself from yanking that hammer out of her grasp and finishing the job—useless as it might be— himself.

Instead, he sighed. "Fine, Wonder Woman, do it yourself if you want—but where in the world did you get that hammer?"

She looked at the toy in her hand. No gloves. Her knuckles were already red from the cold. Her hands seemed soft and fragile—they shouldn't be doing hard labor. It wasn't right. And even if it was—he'd be the first one to admit that, while he could wash dishes with the best of them, he wasn't much of a feminist when it came to women doing dangerous chores—it wasn't *safe*.

"The hammer is from my toolbox," Hailey said. "I bought it as a kit. They said tools for women—specialized."

He shook his head. Helena the kitten wasn't the only one who lacked common sense. "How would you make specialized tools for women?"

"I don't know! I don't know anything about tools, that's the point, but I'm learning. They're the experts. Maybe tools for women mean smaller handles or something?" She spotted an errant nail and headed toward it on her knees.

"Well, in this case they seem to have meant pink. And the hammer's head is about to fall off."

His words were proved right in the vicious swing

she took at the nail. The head fell off, bounced off the icy roof and vanished into a drift of snow below. Hailey was left staring at the pathetic-looking pink handle. ''Dammit!'' she screamed.

The wind was getting worse. If *he* didn't get her down, the storm would. ''Don't worry, you'll find it when the snow thaws.'' He took her arm and tried to guide her toward the ladder, but she resisted. ''Hailey—come on down before the wind blows you down or the cold starts getting to you. You're not dressed well enough.''

''Not yet. This leak is right over my bed, and I just found the hole. I have to fix it or I won't even be able to sleep in there. And I'm up here anyway, so I'm going to finish what I started.''

''Hailey, don't be an idiot! Move your bed. Sleep in another room. Borrow my guest room. Check into a hotel. Anything other than staying up here while the weather is this unpredictable. You won't be able to fix that without proper tools and materials.'' Or without the help of someone who knew what he was doing, but he should probably keep that opinion to himself. Independence was a religion to this woman. ''But you're liable to fall down and break your neck. So am I if I stay up here much longer.'' He reached out again. ''Come on, I'll help you down.''

She slapped his hand away. ''Jordan, listen!''

Snowflakes were caught in her lashes and in the hair escaping from beneath her hat. Her whole face was sparkling. ''I'm listening.''

''I came here to learn to do things on my own.''

''You mean—without Robby?''

She seemed caught off guard, but quickly recovered. "Yes. Exactly. He's away all the time, and I have to adapt to that. I don't need a man to help me out of every scrape I get myself into. I don't *want* a man to help me out."

"Fine, think of me as a St. Bernard, then."

"What?"

"Hailey…" He held out a hand. "What you're doing is dangerous. When the weather clears up, you can get back up here and finish the job. I'll lend you real tools and not even look up on the roof while you're working."

"Real tools?"

"Yes. You can have the run of my garage. Use anything."

She started grinning—and it wasn't a very nice grin. It was pure evil. "Anything? You mean I can play with your power tools?"

He winced. "If you promise to be gentle."

Hailey turned her face into the storm, closing her eyes against the hail beating on her face. "Will the weather *ever* clear up or are we in it for the duration?"

He grinned. "It'll clear up. Sort of."

"Okay. It's a deal."

"Great." He extended a hand. "Let me help you down."

"No. I'll go down, but I can get there by myself. Go home. I'll just gather my tools and go back inside in just a second."

"But—"

"I can handle it. Go! I want to get down on my own."

He sighed. As long as she did get down from here, he was happy. He didn't like leaving her up here instead of helping her down, but if that was the only way…. "Okay. If you decide you want my help after all, just yell."

She didn't answer, and he climbed down the ladder, taking care to wipe the snow off so there'd be less chance of her slipping. He stomped back into his own yard, and used iron will not to turn around and look until he was at his door. To his relief he could see Hailey inching down the ladder.

One crisis averted—but he had a feeling it wouldn't be the last one.

Hailey was fuming when she jumped off the ladder. She turned her face toward Jordan's house, intending to glare at him, but he'd had the sense to vanish inside.

Okay, so it hadn't been the brightest idea to get up there right when the storm was starting up. But he didn't have to be so patronizing, like he knew it all and she knew nothing.

Even if it was undoubtedly true when it came to house repair.

As soon as she was inside, she unzipped her snow-suit as fast as her numb fingers would allow. Of course, she didn't know anything. She hadn't even had the sense to wear gloves. Her fingers were red, numb and starting to hurt like hell now that she was warming up again.

But now she was determined. As soon as the weather improved, she was going back up there to finish what she'd started.

First: a warm bath, warm cocoa and a warm cat to stroke until the wind died down again. She'd reread the DIY book, and then go up there for another attempt.

Whether Jordan liked it or not.

The weather cleared up around noon—but it was only one of those eye-of-the-storm calms, and when he looked out the window, there was Hailey, pulling herself up on the roof again, a sitting snowbunny for when the storm kicked up again. He cursed colorfully as he pulled on his boots and jacket and ran out without even doing up the laces or zipping the jacket. Baby-sitter. Definitely. He'd hire one himself if he had to—it would save him a lot of aggravation.

He climbed the ladder rehearsing a speech in his head, reminding himself not to shout at her. She didn't respond well to shouting. He leaned forward and grabbed her ankle as she was crawling toward the spot she'd been before. ''What the hell are you doing?''

Oops. He'd forgotten not to shout, and as she twisted around to sit there with her legs bent, glaring at him, he knew it had been a mistake.

This time she was wearing gloves, and the snowsuit looked more bulky, meaning she was probably wearing thick sweaters underneath. Good. Maybe the lady did learn from experience, albeit slowly. Her gaze was icier than the weather, though. ''What am I doing? I'd have thought that was obvious. The storm is gone. I'm fixing this hole. What are you doing here?''

''Hailey, the storm isn't over.'' He cursed. ''Look at the clouds all around. They're black. That color give you a hint? It's going to start up again any minute now!''

''I'll go down as soon as it starts blowing again.'' She stood up just as the wind started to kick up again

in a strong gust that had him grappling for hold. Hailey
stumbled. He grabbed her arm and pulled her to safety,
but her foot hit the ladder hard enough to push it to
the side. It teetered for a while, then fell, making no
sound as it landed in the snow almost twenty feet below.

Damn.

"Look what you did!" Hailey shouted, snatching
her arm back and gesturing down at the ladder sunk
deep and rapidly disappearing beneath the snow,
which had started to fall again. "The ladder is gone.
We're stuck up here! Now what do we do?"

"Look what *I* did? Who was it who almost fell off
the roof and kicked the ladder down in the progress?"

Hailey put her hands on her hips. "I was doing just
fine up here. If you hadn't come after me and grabbed
my ankle and started yelling like a madman..."

"You'd probably be lying under that ladder!"

Hailey scowled at him, but let the matter drop. She
glanced around. "Never mind that—how are we going
to get down?"

Jordan made his way carefully to the left side of the
roof and pointed down. "Here's the best spot."

"Best spot for what?"

"Jumping down."

Hailey backed away from him and clutched the
chimney as she sent him an are-you-nuts look. "Jumping down? Are you out of your mind? This is a two-
storey house!"

"Yes, and there is a snowbank there, almost a storey high. It'll be a soft landing."

Hailey peeked down. "It's not safe."

"It is safe. There's no risk of injury, I promise."

"There could be something under there! Hell, they could probably hide a whole garage under there."

He shook his head. "You know there's nothing under there. Just snow. It piles up there because of the trees edging the side against the wind. Come on. Don't think about it too long. Just jump. It's perfectly safe."

Hailey shook her head. Several strands of hair had escaped her hat and danced around her red cheeks. "Absolutely not. There has to be another way down."

"Don't be such a sissy. Jump! Two seconds of free fall, and the softest landing you can imagine."

"Caveman!"

"Let me guess. Your oil rig husband would never ask you to jump down off a roof?"

"Of course he wouldn't! And we have plenty of options! The most obvious one is for you to be a gentleman. Jump by yourself and raise the ladder for me to climb down."

Jordan put his arms around her and held on tight, pulling her away from the chimney, lifting her until her toes didn't touch the ground. He looked into her eyes, wondering why he was finding her stubborn insistence on independence so attractive. It was time to confront her—even if only for the principle of it. "Hailey?"

"Yes?" She braced her hands against his chest and tilted her head back to stare at him warily. "What?"

He grinned at her. "I'm on to you, you know."

She scowled. "On to what?"

His grin widened. "'Fess up. You don't have a husband, do you?"

She bit her lip, then shook her head once. ''No.''

''I knew it.'' Quick, before she had the chance to realize what was happening, he hurled her off the edge.

CHAPTER FOUR

THOSE were the longest two seconds in Hailey's life. She thought she'd never land, but then she did, sinking deep into the bank of fluffy wet snow. For a moment she didn't move, paralyzed with shock, heart slamming against her ribs in belated shock, until a dark shadow approached from above and Jordan landed in the snow beside her. His hand came up to her face. He pushed her hair away from her face, tucked it under her hat, and tilted her head so he could see into her eyes. He was laughing. She'd almost died from fear and he was *laughing*.

"Hailey? We're down. You okay?"

She scrambled to get out of the snow, away from the crazy guy, but the going was tough, even while her system flooded with adrenaline.

"I can't believe you did that," she muttered between clenched teeth, fear and fury driving away all cold. She would have shouted—but her voice wasn't working yet. "Are you crazy? No, don't answer that, you *are* crazy, I don't need to ask! You could have killed both of us!"

"Nonsense." Jordan was just lying in the snow, as comfortable as if he were on a beach. He crossed his arms behind his head to complete the picture and grinned at her. "What's your problem? You couldn't have asked for a safer or more comfortable landing."

"You didn't even wait until I was out of the snow

to jump yourself! You could have jumped on top of me! Your elbow could have hit my eye, my knee could have hit your…kidneys.''

''I knew what I was doing.''

''I am never, ever, in a million years, not even when hell freezes over, ever, *ever* going to forgive you for this!''

''But—''

''And you didn't even *warn* me before *throwing* me off the roof! It was irresponsible, immature, dangerous and *rude!*''

She managed to scream the last word. Good. Her voice was back.

''If I'd asked if I could throw you off the roof, you'd have said no, right?''

''Yes!''

''So there was no point in asking, was there?''

Hailey shook her head. ''You're unbelievable.''

''We didn't have a lot of options, did we?''

''Yes.'' Hailey slammed a hand into the snow and resisted the temptation to grab a handful and thrust it under his collar. His down jacket was open, revealing only a checkered shirt underneath. He had to be freezing. ''You could have jumped on your own, like I suggested!''

The twinkle in Jordan's eyes told her this wasn't a news flash to him. ''Yes. I could have. But that wouldn't have been nearly as much fun.''

''Fun?''

He finally pulled himself to a sitting position, and helped her climb out of their icy nest.

''Yes. Fun. Besides, you deserved a punishment after lying to me about having a husband.''

"It was a functional lie! A tiny functional lie that hurt nobody. I don't owe people the truth about the details of my life, do I? As long as I'm honest about who I am, the precise details shouldn't matter." This was what she'd been telling herself, anyway. But it had started to dawn on her, that perhaps who she was depended to a large extent on those little details.

"Functional lie? What is that, a euphemism for a white lie? White lies are politically incorrect now?"

"The lie was functional. Practical. It served a purpose and didn't hurt anyone. It prevents a lot of misunderstandings."

"Such as?"

"Why are we talking about this?"

"You're the one who lied."

"Because I want people to think I'm unavailable."

"I see."

"Yes. It was necessary. People back home kept trying to set me up. I didn't want that to continue. I don't date. I don't want anybody to think I'm available because I'm not."

"You can just say no, you know."

Ah. There was the rub. She should be able to say no…but that resolve had never lasted very long. That was why she'd decided to flee her home—so that she'd have a better chance of lasting out the year. "Theoretically, yes."

"But…?"

"But it's much easier if I can just get the message across once and for all. I'm not available."

"You're not?"

"Nope. So I'm not interested in being set up, or

being asked out, or having anything to do with guys, and if people think I'm married, they won't push me.''

''Why aren't you interested?''

Why was she discussing this? Why with him? She looked up at the dark sky. And why in the middle of a snowstorm?

But, well, he'd wormed out her secret. Now her only chance was to convince him to keep it a secret, and for that he'd probably need the whole story.

She'd try the easy way first. ''It's a long, boring story that you couldn't possibly want to hear. The short version—I discovered I don't like men very much.''

''Oh.'' He was taken aback. ''You mean... Oh, sorry. I didn't realize.''

''No!'' She was sure she was blushing now. Her cheeks were already red from the cold, but the color was probably spreading. ''I do like *men*. I just don't *like* men.''

''The difference being...?''

''If I wanted to date, I would date men. But I don't want to date, so I'm not dating anyone. Male, female or neuter.''

''I see.'' A particularly nasty gust of wind grabbed at them, and he put his arm over her shoulders, dragging her with him to the relative shelter of the back porch. ''No love-life at all, huh?''

''Nope.'' She stomped her feet, ridding her boots of most of the snow. A lot had gone inside them too, while scrambling out of the snow. They'd probably take forever to dry. ''You have no idea how much that has simplified my life. I didn't even bring any panty hose with me to Alaska.''

"Are you telling me women wear panty hose for men?"

She rubbed her forehead with the back of her glove, realizing too late that she'd probably left a big muddy mark. "Well...no, but.... Well, anyway, I haven't worn any for months now. No skirts either. I've turned into a tomboy in my old age, and I like it."

He nodded. "Men prefer stockings, anyway. Panty hose don't do much for us, you know. Stockings are about a million times more alluring."

She snorted, even though she noticed the teasing glint in his eyes. Pulling her leg—no pun intended—or not, of course his mind would still be on the panty hose. "Garters and all, I guess. Men! Sheesh, why not just wrap us up in cellophane and a red ribbon and be done with it?"

He grinned at her. "Excellent idea. You're right. We'd like that."

"Well..." She looked at him uncertainly. "I've been getting vibes from you. And just so we're straight on this, I'm not sending any vibes back."

He looked startled for a while, then recovered enough to send her a slow, confident grin. "Liar."

This wasn't going right at all. When had she lost control of the situation? Probably around the time she got thrown off the roof. "Are you calling me a liar?"

"I'm getting vibes too, you know." He moved again, and it seemed to bring him closer, but it hadn't. He'd just shifted so that his back was to the wind, protecting her from the snow blowing into her face. It was only the intensity in his eyes that reached out to her. But she backed away anyway.

"Nope. No vibes. I'm not transmitting at all."

"Liar, Hailey. The vibes are coming in waves."

"Well, it's not vibes. Has to be random interference in the air. Elecromagnetic interference."

"Really?"

"Solar storms," she added desperately. "It doesn't mean anything."

He finally zipped up his jacket and slid his hands into the pockets. Maybe he wasn't impervious to the cold after all. "Don't worry, you're quite safe. Vibes or not, I'm not even remotely interested, so we'll be fine."

Hailey stared at him. "Ouch! That was *rude*."

"Wasn't it what you wanted to hear?"

"In principle, yes, but did it ever cross your mind to let a lady down easy?"

"*Lady?* Funny, I wouldn't have thought Ms. I-can-fix-the-roof-myself would be thinking of herself as a *lady*."

"That's where you're wrong. That's where most men are wrong. Feminism and femininity are not mutually exclusive!"

He nodded. "Okay. Got it. But don't worry, *lady,* you're safe with me."

She had to ask, didn't she? "Why?"

"I'm not getting involved with an out-of-towner, no matter what. Not interested. At all."

"Really?"

"Yup."

Hailey put her hands on her hips, feeling chagrined. She wanted to ask why, but that might indicate interest. Above and beyond the reluctant interest her wayward vibes had already communicated, of course.

"Not interested *at all,* huh? You're seriously messing with my self-esteem here, you know."

"What's the problem? I thought you wanted men to stay away from you?"

"Yes. I want them to stay away from me because they're afraid of my big strong husband. Not because they're *not interested at all!*"

Jordan grinned. "Okay. If you were a born-and-bred Alaskan, I would be all over you. That feed your self-esteem?"

"What sort of statism is that, anyway?"

"Statism?"

"You know, like racism or sexism. Are you discriminating against me because I'm from another state?"

"No. But I have my kid to think about first. I'm staying in Alaska because he's here, and I can't leave—I *won't* leave—until he's off to college."

"Oh."

"Yeah. And in the meantime I'm not taking any risks of getting tangled up in something. So outsiders are strictly off limits to me." He pointed at her. "Which rules you out."

"I see."

"Feeling better?"

She straightened. "Absolutely. Apart from that little rule, you want me *bad,* don't you?"

He grinned at her teasing tone, just as he was supposed to, and things looked better already. This could be great. The terms were clear—they might even be able to become friends.

Her smile faded. No. She could not be friends with a man—certainly not one she was attracted to. Been there, done that. Too risky. "Just friends" never worked. It was a line guys used, a trap.

Jordan wasn't reading her mind. He held out a hand. "Since we've got our lack of intentions straightened out—how about we become friends instead?"

She took a step back. "No!"

Jordan's hand fell to the side and his eyebrows rose. "No? Okay."

Damn! "I mean, it might not work. Us being friends. What if…"

"Hailey, I'm not talking about a lifetime commitment here. It was just a casual question."

"We can be friends in the 'friendly neighbor' fashion. But no getting drunk together or anything like that. And we don't bring our heartbreak stories to each other, okay? People on the rebound are dangerous. And we don't spend a lot of time in each other's houses, either. Just outdoors."

"No alcohol, no rebounds, no indoors. Check. Anything else?"

"No. Not at the moment."

"Then we can be friends?"

She grinned, knowing how silly she was acting, but not really caring. If he thought she was nuts, all the better. "Right. Friends."

He grinned as he took her hand. "I think this is going to be the weirdest friendship I have ever had. But this does mean you've forgiven me for tossing you off the roof, right?"

She withdrew her hand and frowned. "Well, that's pushing it. It's not the kind of thing friends do to one another, is it?"

"Didn't you ever jump down into a pile of snow as a kid?"

"I'm a California baby. I was eighteen before I saw snow."

"Poor thing. Nothing beats a jump off a high surface and landing in a soft pile of snow. I could spend an entire day doing that when I was Simon's age."

She scoffed. "Nothing beats that? You've never been to Disneyland, have you?"

Jordan climbed out of the snow and grabbed her upper arms to pull her up. "No."

"Much better than jumping off roofs," she said, then looked up on the roof, frowning. "Dammit, I left my tool kit up there."

"No problem. I'll go get it."

"I'll go—" she started saying, but he had already raised the ladder and climbed it. A few moments later her toolbox landed in a pile of snow, and then Jordan landed right beside it.

Hailey leaned forward to get her box, then held out a hand to help him out of the snowdrift. "Thanks," she said grudgingly. "Although I could have—"

"—done it yourself. I know." He grinned as he took her hand, but she slipped and landed facedown in the snow beside him.

"Hi," he said, blinking at her as she turned her face and spat out snow. "We've got to stop meeting like this."

"Great. A veterinarian and a comedian," Hailey muttered, crawling out of the snow. "Irresistible mixture."

"Yeah, I get that all the time," Jordan said. "Will

you give up working on that roof now? Please? For the sake of my sanity?''

''Yes,'' she said with a sigh. ''I'll postpone it.''

''Just how bad is it in there?''

''Bad.''

''Show me.''

Hailey hesitated, then shrugged. ''Sure. Come on.''

It was bad. Her bed was shoved to the side and a large half-filled bucket of water was sitting where her pillow should be. That pillow had been thrown in a plastic tub, sopping wet. Water still dripped from the ceiling.

''Oh, boy,'' Jordan muttered.

''Yeah. I already called Jane. She said it was bad last year—but not this bad. She said she'd talk to the landlord for me—but I just wanted to do something to fix the worst of it.''

''This is not something you can fix in a few minutes up on the roof.'' He shook his head. ''I've got a spare room—Simon's room. You're welcome to stay there if you want.''

''Thanks for the offer, but I'll be fine downstairs.''

''That tiny old sofa? It's not big enough, even for you!''

''I'll be fine,'' she repeated, lifting her chin in a stubborn manner that was becoming familiar.

He shrugged. ''Well, if you change your mind, just come knocking.''

Hailey shuffled her feet as she stood there on Jordan's doorstep, duffel bag in hand. ''Okay, so you were right. It's not possible to sleep on that sofa.''

''I'm not surprised.''

"Don't get me wrong—I called around. Did you know there's only one hotel in town, and it's closed most of the year?"

Jordan grinned. "Yeah."

"Well—since it's only for the night, I'd like to take you up on that offer of a guest room—but only if you promise not to say I told you so."

Jordan kept grinning as he opened the door wider. "No problem."

"Just for the night," she stressed. "I know Mrs. Crumbs from school will be more than happy to put me up for a few days if I need to… but it's too late to call her now."

"You're welcome to stay here. Simon's room is available. Think you can survive the dogs? They seem to love you more than you love them."

Hailey stiffened when the dogs approached her. She'd always felt safer with them on the other side of the fence. She liked animals, she just wasn't used to them—but those were some big dogs. "I think I'll survive. Will Helena be okay?"

"The cat? You brought Helena with you?"

"Of course." She reached inside her coat and held up the animal. "I could hardly leave her behind all alone, could I? Will your dogs gobble her up?"

"Nah. They're used to her. Usually, they ignore her. She tends to take offense at that."

Hailey allowed the kitten to jump to the floor. She instantly approached the dogs, circling them, patting their feet with her paws, but neither of them seemed to notice her.

"I can see why she doesn't like that," Hailey mused. "She likes to be the center of attention." She looked around, then toward the door. "Will people talk? About me staying here?"

"I'm not telling if you're not. We'll pull the drapes and nobody will be the wiser."

She grimaced. "I don't know. I've found people are awfully good at finding things out, and equally quick to jump to conclusions."

Jordan nodded as he took her coat. "I know. Seven years since Simon was born and my reputation still hasn't recovered."

"Oh."

He led the way to the living room and gave her a pointed look. "Don't tell me you haven't heard the rumors?"

She squirmed. "I don't like to listen to gossip…"

"But sometimes gossip has a way of infiltrating anyway… I know. Coffee?"

She shook her head. "Not this late, thank you."

"Beer?"

She thought for a moment, then shrugged. "Sure, why not? I'll live dangerously!"

Male company was a nice change, Hailey admitted, although she didn't want to admit it. She wasn't breaking her resolution, though, or the rules for their friendship. Okay, so they were indoors, but the rule had called for "not a lot of time" indoors. This qualified as an emergency, and didn't count. Jordan knew her rules—he had rules of his own. He was just a helpful neighbor.

But it was a nice change to hear masculine laughter, the deep timbre of his voice. She'd always liked being around men. Maybe that was one of her problems.

Jordan seemed to be reading her mind. Or her face—she suspected the thought had made her frown. "Tell me more about this 'I don't like men' thing of yours," he said, shifting in the sofa and reaching out for a beer bottle. "I mean—have you sworn men off for good?"

"Oh, no. Not for good. One year." She held up a finger. "One year of being on my own, without even thinking about men. To break a bad habit—to prove to myself I can do it."

"Then what?"

She shrugged. "I hope I'll have a different outlook on life—and then we'll see."

Jordan swung the bottle back and forth by its neck. "Why are you doing this? Did something happen?"

Hailey grimaced. "No major trauma, really, although heartbreak always feels like a major trauma at the time, doesn't it? Just one loser too many and a realization that I was bringing this on myself."

"How so?"

"What are you, my therapist?"

He grinned. "Sorry. Never mind. Didn't mean to pry."

"No, it's okay. I miss my girlfriends. You can stand in for them."

"Oh, great."

"We're not braiding each other's hair anymore, so don't worry." Hailey reached out for her own beer bottle. She'd never much liked beer before, but it sort of seemed to go with the territory here. "The thing is—I think I'm addicted to being in a relationship. Any kind of relationship."

"Addicted? Isn't that a bit strong?"

She nodded. "Yes—but it's the truth. Whenever I wasn't in a relationship I'd feel incomplete, like there was something wrong with me, something missing. So I'd rush into a relationship—and of course, it would fail. So, I figured I needed time off. Cold turkey."

"Interesting. How is it going?"

"Great. Wonderful. Forty weeks down, only twelve to go, and I haven't even looked sideways at a man."

"No?"

"Well, barely," she confessed, feeling guilty about some of the not-quite-prim-and-proper thoughts she'd had over the last few weeks—most of them about the man across the coffee table. "Maybe I've *looked,* but that's it. I mean... I can look, can't I? If there's some extraordinary specimen. I mean, one does not pass a perfect rose without casting a glance at it, right?"

He rubbed his face with his hand, without much luck trying to conceal the grin. "Right," he said. "A perfect rose, a perfect guy—you're absolutely right, one just has to stop and take a look."

"You're making fun of me, aren't you?"

"Yes, I am." He stood up. "Let me show you Simon's room."

Simon's room was a typical little boy's room, although considerably neater than usual, probably because the occupant only spent every other weekend in this house. Jordan gathered the bedclothes and threw them in a hamper before fetching new ones from a closet.

"You don't mind cartoon covers, do you?" he asked.

"Superheroes? No. I love superheroes. I adore superheroes!"

He looked over his shoulder from where he was pulling pillows out of a top shelf. "Let me guess. You had a crush on Superman as a little girl, right?"

She smiled wistfully. "Yes. That may be the core of my problems. My standard was set by Superman."

CHAPTER FIVE

To: Ellen
From: Hailey@MySelfImposedExile.com
Subject: Men!

Men! You're not going to believe this! I got up on that roof yesterday, and a big macho Alaskan comes and throws me down!

I was *so* mad. But I'm still proud of myself for giving it a try and then defying him—at least in theory. A year ago, I would have smiled meekly and climbed down the ladder as soon as someone told me to. Well, no more!

Of course, he did get me off the roof, but he had to use his superior physical strength to bodily throw me down. It may not sound like much of a victory, but trust me, it is.

Anyway, the roof is in worse shape than I thought. My landlord is actually going to do something about it, but I'll be staying with a colleague for a couple of days, so I won't be answering the phone. I have e-mail access at school though, so keep them coming.

Love,
Hailey, born-again feminist

One night in Jordan's house was quite enough for someone doing spinster-for-a-year. Meeting him in the hallway in the morning, sleepy-looking, barefoot and bare-chested with unsnapped jeans, had stopped her breathing for too many seconds. Of course, learning to deal with temptation was part of her new life plan—but there was temptation and then there was *temptation.*

Mrs. Crumbs to the rescue.

Hyacinth Crumbs lived just two streets away, in a big house crammed with much-loved furniture from several different decades. Several of her grandchildren lived close by, so the yard was crowded with snow figures and her children's childhood rooms were still filled with toys getting regular workouts. Hailey got "the girl room"—Mrs. Crumbs had four boys and only one girl.

"It was a chaotic household," Mrs. Crumbs explained happily as she checked the shelves for dust. "And then my Lynn might just as well have been another boy—she abhorred dresses, pretended her dolls were cowboys and Indians, and I could never get bows to stick in her hair longer than ten minutes. Oh, dear, it's been a while since I've dusted this room, hasn't it?"

"Nonsense. And anyway, I'm used to dust," Hailey assured her. "The room is perfect. I really appreciate you helping me out."

Mrs. Crumbs' brow wrinkled even further. "You're used to dust from Jane's house? She's such a neat girl…"

"No, not Jane, it's me. I'm not the best housekeeper around. And living alone, well, sometimes there seems little point in keeping up the dust defense."

Mrs. Crumbs chuckled. "So I suppose you do quick cleanups just before Mr. Rutherford comes home?"

Hailey nearly closed her eyes in shame. *Living alone.* How could she have forgotten about poor far-away Robby again? "Yes. Something like that."

Oh, God. They better fix that roof soon. The rough estimate had been two weeks, and she really hoped they were exaggerating. She'd break down and squeal soon, if Mrs. Crumbs kept up her interrogations about Robby.

The next week, it was time for Hailey's class to visit Jordan's clinic. He came to talk to the kids the day before, and she could stay at the back of the class-room, watching him perch on the edge of her desk looking more scrumptious than any man had a right to.

It wasn't fair!

The kids rushed out for their recess, some of them pausing to ask Jordan a question, but finally the class-room was empty. He grinned at her from across the room. "I take it my talk didn't impress you very much?"

"What do you mean?"

"You were frowning at me the entire time."

"Oh." Oops. "I'm sorry—that had nothing to do with your talk. My mind was on something else."

"Marital issues?" he asked blandly. The twinkle in his eye could have lit up a ballroom.

She made a face at him. "Give it a rest, will you? Coming to the teachers' lounge?"

"Sure." He followed her out the door. "Helena misses you," he said. "She can't understand why you're not opening the door when she scratches it."

"Poor thing." Oh, damn, more guilt. "I've gone over there twice this week, hoping to see her, but she was nowhere to be found."

"She's indoors most of the time. Usually she can be found on a windowsill over a radiator. Next time, if I'm not home yet, just walk on in and say hello to her."

Hailey shook her head hard. She'd never get used to this way of thinking. "I will not 'just walk on in' to a stranger's house!"

"I'm hardly a stranger," he protested. "You have an open invitation. Drop by anytime."

Hailey almost shuddered. "I couldn't. I just couldn't walk into someone else's house like that. Goes against the grain."

"What's the problem? You've already spent the night there."

"Sssssh!" Hailey hissed. "Keep your voice down! And *no*, I'm not just walking into your house if you're not there."

Jordan chuckled. "Fine. Call first, then, to see if I'm home. I'm almost always home by six or so."

"Will do."

"How's staying with Hyacinth?"

"Fine. I think I'm gaining two pounds a day from her cooking, but she's a wonderful host."

They made it to the teachers' lounge and Hailey piled her paperwork on a table. "How are the workers doing?" she asked him. "Making a lot of noise, I presume? Have you had to rescue anyone off the roof lately?"

He chuckled. "No. But one of them found your pink hammer."

"Goodie."

"There was much rejoicing."

"I can imagine."

"You might be able to go home this weekend. The workers said they were about finished."

"Great! That's ahead of schedule—they planned to be done middle of next week. I'm impressed."

"The foreman is Mrs. Crumbs' son-in-law. Apparently she's been putting pressure on him."

"Oh." Had she outstayed her welcome at Mrs. Crumbs'? "I guess I've been imposing…"

"I don't think it's that she wants you out of the house. She's worried that you don't want to call Siberia from her house and are losing touch with Robby."

"I see." Hailey glanced furtively around, although he hadn't really said anything that would blow her cover. Mrs. Crumbs was approaching, full speed.

"I love having you!" Mrs. Crumbs protested indignantly, glaring at Jordan for having suggested otherwise. She'd been standing halfway across the room, but obviously forty years of disciplining ten-year-olds had sharpened her hearing. "I just want you to get home as soon as possible, so you'll feel more free to contact your husband."

"Thank you, I appreciate all your help."

Mrs. Crumbs shook her head. "I just wish you'd feel free to use my phone to call your husband. One or two international phone calls won't bankrupt me— and you can pay me back as soon as I get my itemized bill." She was distracted by some shouting from the corridor, and raised her own voice to that calm thunder that had even the most hardened fifth-graders cowering. "Anne and Elizabeth, stop that right now!"

She was off, and Hailey leaned against the wall, feeling drained. "I had no idea lying was so exhausting," she whispered, after checking around to see if anyone was within earshot. "Really—I'm exhausted from constantly keeping in mind that I'm a married woman with a hunk of a husband somewhere off the coast of Siberia."

Jordan was chuckling. She glared at him, but it didn't work; his chuckle morphed into full-blown laughter. Why in the world was it that laughter creases made men so utterly attractive, but women had to spend a fortune trying—in vain—to stave their own wrinkles off? It was so unfair.

"What?"

He held out his hands in a gesture of innocence, but kept grinning. "Don't look at me, I'm just an amused bystander."

"It's not funny."

"Are you kidding? It's hilarious. I can't wait to see how you're going to worm your way out of this." He shook his head with a bemused expression. "This can't go on forever, you know."

"It doesn't have to. I'm leaving soon—dilemma solved."

"The run-and-hide strategy, huh?"

"You bet. I've used it in the past with much success."

"Who have you been running away from?"

"None of your business."

"You're going to leave your web of lies behind for the rest of us to trip through?"

She shrugged. "It's the only way. You'll forget me soon enough."

Jordan gave her a lopsided grin. "Don't count on that, *Mrs.* Rutherford."

"Mr. Rutherford hasn't been in touch at all the entire week." Friday evening, Mrs. Crumbs' lined face radiated a fine balance of altruistic concern and gossipy curiosity. "Didn't you give him this phone number? It's quite okay for him to call here."

"It's okay, Hyacinth, really—we e-mail back and forth a lot, and save the phone calls for special occasions. E-mail is so much cheaper."

"How do they have an Internet connection out there?"

Good question. How did an oil rig have an Internet connection? Didn't Internet connections always rely on some sort of a cable connection? It didn't just go through the air like radio, did it?

God, she felt so ignorant sometimes. "Uh...I have to admit I'm not quite sure..."

"They can't have any cables to shore, can they? Or could they be linked to an oceanic cable?"

"I really don't know..."

Mrs. Crumbs snapped her fingers. "I know! Satellite! That has to be it."

"Maybe." She seized the explanation gratefully. "That could be it. I've never even wondered. Just took it for granted."

"Maybe you could ask him next time you talk? I'm quite curious about how these things work."

"Sure, I'll try to remember to ask him." Damn. More things to research. She'd have to make use of all this knowledge someday. Perhaps a thematic month with her third-graders at home next year: "Life on an Oil Rig."

It sounded like Mrs. Crumbs had already snapped up that idea. "You know, my class is quite interested in this oil rig thing. They've been asking a lot of questions. Maybe you could come sometime for a Q and A?"

"I really don't think that would be a good idea," Hailey hurried to say. "I don't know all that much about the subject myself. I've never even seen an oil rig."

"Nonsense. Even what little you've picked up from your husband about daily life there is much more than any of us know. Another idea. Maybe Mr. Rutherford could call in and we could have an intercom conference." Mrs. Crumbs sounded delighted. "Wouldn't that be a wonderful use of technology? The kids would be ecstatic! Okay, so it's not a satellite link to the International Space Station, which is what they really want, but it's the next best thing."

"I really don't think that would work…. The connection is really bad, not very reliable…"

Mrs. Crumbs nodded sagely. "Satellites can be temperamental, I suppose. But mention it to him, dear, never hurts. You said he loved kids, he might quite enjoy this."

"Sure. I'll mention it to him." She tried to sound enthusiastic and positive, but failed. God! This was becoming increasingly complicated. It would almost be easier to confess to everything rather than keep stacking lie upon lie in a precarious house of cards.

Houses of cards always tumbled, unless you cheated and used glue.

Unfortunately, all the glue in the universe wouldn't hold this one together for much longer. But then it didn't have to last much more than a couple of months, till she went home.

Mrs. Crumbs was looking at her, eyes narrowed all of a sudden. Hailey felt a pang of panic. She suspected. Dammit, Mrs. Crumbs suspected something. "Dear—are your hands still swollen? Can I take a look?" Without waiting for an answer, she took Hailey's hands and inspected them, first palms up, then palms down. "Don't look swollen anymore. Have you tried your wedding ring on lately? I'm sure it fits now."

"I'll try it out and see," Hailey said weakly. Mrs. Crumbs nodded, and busied herself with the espresso machine. What now? Would she have to travel to the city to buy herself a wedding ring? There was a jeweler in town, but with the gossip level around here she'd be found out in a microsecond. And what kind of a ring would she be buying? Knowing good old Robby, it would be a fancy, expensive one—a ring to last a lifetime and beyond. Tasteful, of course, nothing overly flashy or gaudy, but expensive.

She couldn't afford something like that. Did they make good fake jewelry these days?

What had she tangled herself into? Surely buying an actual wedding ring was going too far. But if Mrs. Crumbs suspected she was lying about her husband...

Nerves frayed, she jumped as the phone rang. "Could you get that for me, dear?" Mrs. Crumbs called out, and Hailey picked up the phone. It was

Jordan—and a sudden flash of desperate inspiration struck.

"Hi, darling!" she called joyfully. "What a wonderful surprise!"

Jordan went silent. She pretended to cover the phone with her hand, but made sure Jordan would hear as she called to Mrs. Crumbs. "It's Robby—I'll take it in the other room, okay?"

"By all means—close the door for privacy!" Mrs. Crumbs beamed at her, and Hailey snuck into the family room, closing the door behind her.

"What are you doing, Hailey?" Jordan asked. She wasn't sure if he was sounding amused or irritated. "How in the world is this going to help? Aren't you in deep enough trouble as it is?"

"Oh, no, not at all."

"Do you have to get me in trouble as well?"

"Well, you know, misery loves company."

"Hyacinth was my teacher, you know. I still can't lie to her."

Hailey stared at the door, wondering how easily voices carried through the thin wood. "Darling, it's been so long! It's wonderful to hear your voice again. How are you?"

Jordan laughed. "I take it you think Hyacinth is listening at the door? That would be rather rude of her, even in her own home."

Hailey made an effort to put love and tenderness and yearning into her voice, and an even stronger effort to not think about what she was doing. She had a nagging feeling this had been one of her worst ideas so far—but it was too late to back out. "I miss you too, my love. I can't wait for Christmas."

"Speaking of Christmas, what will you really be doing over the holidays? Home with Mom and Dad, waiting out the last days of your self-imposed spinsterhood, ready to jump the first man you see after midnight on New Year's Eve?"

She laughed shyly, as if he'd said something outrageous yet pleasing, but rolling her eyes at herself. This was absurd! What had she been thinking? But too late now. Nothing to do but soldier on. The thought injected just the right amount of exasperation into her voice and she tempered it with another laugh. "Robby!"

"You'll be a free woman as soon as the clock strikes midnight. It should be interesting."

What the hell was he talking about? Why did he care what she'd be doing on New Year's Eve anyway? "Oh, yes. I can't wait either."

"A reverse Cinderella," he mused. "Surrounded by handsome princes waiting for her to wake from her coma."

"You're mixing up your fairy tales, my love."

"You're right. You believe you'll be surrounded by nothing but scumbag frogs, don't you?"

"Well, there is that."

"Ever heard of something called self-fulfilling prophecy?"

"Oh, Robby sweetheart, you always know just the right thing to say."

Jordan snorted, sounding aggressive and annoyed all of a sudden. "You know, I like this Robby character less and less with every week that passes. The guy's just a little *too* perfect, you know. You have to give him some flaws."

Hailey saw a shadow passing under the door. Mrs. Crumbs might or might not be listening out there, but she probably had an excellent excuse to be so close to the door. "There, there, darling. No need to be jealous, you know you're the only man for me."

Whoa. Where had that come from? She wasn't flirting, was she? She wasn't allowed to flirt for ten more weeks. An uncomfortable feeling gnawed at her stomach. Only ten weeks to go. She wouldn't let herself down now. She couldn't do that to herself.

Jordan was laughing again, a rich, warm sound filled with humor and even affection. That wasn't helping. "You're nuts, Hailey. I've enjoyed watching you put on this show—but I have no idea how you've gotten away with it. It must be either pure genius or dumb luck."

She resisted the temptation to stick her tongue out at him. Not because it was childish, but because he wouldn't be able to see it over the phone. "Did you just call to hear my voice, sweetheart, or was there something in particular you wanted to talk to me about?"

"Right. I almost forgot. Your house is ready. You can move back in tonight if you want."

"That's great!" She didn't have to fake her enthusiasm this time and had to force her mouth shut to keep from asking for details. Like…just how bad did things look?

Jordan read her mind. "A lot of their equipment is still here, and the outside is pretty messy. Not sure in what state they left the inside. They'll be doing the last cleanup on Monday, but they said you'd be fine moving in if you wanted to."

"Wonderful!"

"I take it Hyacinth is still listening?"

"Uh-huh. Think so."

Jordan made a sound of pretend sympathy. "Do you want me to make kissing sounds or something? I bet that's something Robby would do."

She gritted her teeth. He deserved a snowball attack at the earliest convenient opportunity. "I'll call you soon, darling. I miss you. Yes. I love you too. 'Bye."

"Wait!"

"What?" she nearly hissed. Making fake declarations of love wasn't helping her mood. It felt *wrong*. "Yes, darling?" she added in a syrupy voice for Mrs. Crumbs' sake.

"Are you coming home tonight?"

"Yes."

"So I guess I should call you again, as myself this time, to tell you the news about the house."

She hadn't thought of that. There were quite a lot of things she hadn't thought of, weren't there? "Good thinking, darling, thank you. That would be great."

He chuckled. "I kind of like it when you call me all those cute names, *sweetie*. Makes me feel all warm and fuzzy inside."

"Don't get too used to it, *my angel*."

He laughed. "You're nuts, Hailey." He hung up and she was left with a dial tone.

She sighed aloud as she pasted a glowing smile on her face and breezed through the door to tell Mrs. Crumbs more lies about Robby. At least Mrs. Crumbs couldn't doubt his existence anymore. Her secret was safe for a while.

But damn. As if Jordan wasn't finding this whole

thing amusing enough as it was, without being cast in the role of Robby. Why didn't he like Robby, anyway? What was there not to like?

"Good news?" Mrs. Crumbs asked. "Not that I was eavesdropping, but I couldn't help but overhearing a word here and there—sounded like he had some good news for you."

"Yes." Hailey practiced her brightest smile again, trying to look like a woman deliriously in love with the most wonderful man in the known universe. "He's coming home sooner than anticipated. Isn't it great?"

"That's terrific! Will he be coming here, then? There are so many people who would love to meet him."

"No, we'll be meeting in California, but he'll be several days ahead of schedule. For once, he'll be there to help with the Christmas shopping."

"I've found men to be a hindrance rather than help with such things," Mrs. Crumbs complained. "And all my daughters-in-law agree. But maybe your Robby is different."

"He certainly is!" Hailey confirmed with a smile.

CHAPTER SIX

A SHORT while later Mrs. Crumbs answered the phone, chatting with Jordan for quite a while before hanging up without even calling Hailey. "It was Jordan," she said. "You can move back already tonight."

"Really? That's great!"

"I invited Jordan to dinner with us—then he can drive you back."

"Oh, I could walk, that's not a problem. It's only a few minutes' walk."

"You've got a lot of things here—it could be cumbersome to carry. Don't look a gift neighbor in the mouth! There's a free home-cooked meal in it for him—a bachelor knows better than to turn down an offer like that."

Thank God for Mrs. Crumbs' three cats and one dog. With Mrs. Crumbs seeking Jordan's opinion on everything from their food to the likelihood of permanent trauma to being stuck in the cat flap, Hailey could contribute with a few comments about Helena, but Robby was mercifully kept out of the picture. Still, the possibility had her nerves on edge and she breathed a sigh of relief after dinner when Mrs. Crumbs shooed Jordan upstairs to take a look at her cats while she and Hailey did the dishes.

"How lovely that Robby called," Mrs. Crumbs mused. "He must be lonely over there, seeing you so rarely."

"Yes. But he has his friends. And we're used to this. We make good use of our time together."

"Tell me, dear, are there any…women on these oil rigs?"

Good question. Were there? Hailey squirted soap into a pot and cursed herself for not doing more oil rig research, then realized what worried Mrs. Crumbs. "Oh, I don't have to worry about that. Robby could be surrounded by the most beautiful women in the world but he would never cheat on me. He *loves* me. He'd never hurt me."

"It can be difficult for a man to be away from his woman for such a long time."

"No more so than for the woman," Hailey bristled. Then she winked. "Don't worry. I have my ways to keep him in line. I send him e-mails to remind him what he's missing and what he can expect when he gets back."

Mrs. Crumbs cackled in delight. "I love young women today," she confided. "I wish I'd had the nerve to send Mr. Crumbs sexy letters."

"What in the world are you two talking about?"

Jordan's voice, brimming with amusement, boomed from behind and Hailey nearly splashed Mrs. Crumbs with hot soapy water.

"Hailey knows how to keep her husband in line," Mrs. Crumbs informed him. "Cybersex."

"*What?* No, wait a minute, I didn't say—"

"I've read about it and I think it's an excellent thing for a young couple stranded on opposite sides of the world. Much better than straying, that's for sure."

Jordan looked between them, but Hailey turned back to the sink and refused to meet his eyes. Then he coughed, seemingly in lieu of actually saying something. Oh, God. How had this happened?

"Cyber…"

"Yes," Mrs. Crumbs confirmed. "Sexy e-mails written in the nude to remind him what's waiting for him at home. A most excellent idea, I think."

Hailey saw stars. She didn't see much else because her eyes were squeezed shut, and she didn't think she'd be opening them anytime soon. How had an innocent remark about scintillating e-mails turned into cybersex? "No! I didn't say anything about *nude!* Who would write e-mails in the nude?"

"I see," Jordan drawled. "Marital cybersex. Interesting. Maybe they should add that to the marriage vows. 'With my keyboard I thee worship.'"

Her face was flaming now. She wasn't sure if it was the cybersex part or having Jordan witness her so blatantly lying to a kind, old lady who was putting a roof over her head.

Mrs. Crumbs patted her hand. "I'm sorry, dear, I embarrassed you. It's not easy, you know, keeping up with two centuries. Even with seven teenage grandchildren, it's sometimes hard for an old woman to realize when she's being hip and modern and when she's sounding utterly senile and obnoxious. I'm sorry."

"I do *not* write e-mails in the nude," Hailey muttered, not sure why she was intent on establishing that fact. "Heck, because of that lousy roof, I've had to wear two sweaters just to keep warm in that house."

"What you and your husband do in the privacy of your own e-mails is none of our business anyway," Mrs. Crumbs said. "I should never have mentioned it.

Jordan, you're a gentleman, aren't you? I trust you will forget you heard anything about this.''

She was using her teacher's voice, and Jordan snapped to attention like he was still in the fifth grade. ''I'll do my best, ma'am.''

They helped Mrs. Crumbs clean up after dinner, then ferried Hailey's stuff from the guest room. Mrs. Crumbs had been right—there was much more stuff here than she'd have been able to carry in one trip. It filled most of the back of Jordan's truck.

''Don't say it,'' Hailey muttered as they pulled out of the driveway and Mrs. Crumbs was out of sight. ''Just don't.''

''Wasn't going to.''

''Good.''

''Hyacinth is right. What you and Mr. Perfect do in the privacy of your own e-mails…''

''Oh, shut up!''

''You know, Mr. Rutherford is turning into quite a celebrity around town. I hear this guy does just about everything but turn water into wine.''

''Not my fault if people gossip.''

''Speaks five languages, doesn't he? And brings home bonsai trees he nurtures in his tiny oil rig cabin.''

She slid down in her seat. ''Stop it.''

''Bonsai trees! What kind of a guy would spend his time nurturing bonsai trees on an oil rig in Siberia when he could be at home with a wife like you?''

''I'll take that as a compliment.''

''You're going too far, Hailey.''

''I know. No objections from me. This wasn't

planned, you know. It just happened, and I don't know how to pull back.''

''You can't pull back. You either stick with the lie or make a full confession.''

''I know.''

''Are you going to confess?''

''And expose myself as an utter nut and a compulsive liar? Hardly.''

''You've dug a nice pit for yourself, haven't you?''

''Why do you sound so cheerful about it?''

He grinned at her. ''It's sort of fun to watch.''

''I'm your son's teacher. Aren't you worried about moral corruption?''

''No. I've watched you slide down that slope. I know the tiny lie you started with and the reason behind it. I think you are a nut, but an adorable one, not a psycho.''

''Gee, thanks.''

''Are you going to tell me what that phone call was all about? Why was it so important to prove Robby's existence all of a sudden? Did she suspect something?''

Hailey squirmed. Talking on the phone had been one thing, but now, alone with him, she was feeling stupid about the whole thing again. ''Yes.''

''And?''

''Now she doesn't.''

''Well, you're welcome,'' he drawled.

''It's the lack of a wedding ring. People seem to put so much stock in a wedding ring. I really don't want to compound the lie by going to the lengths of buying an actual ring...''

"The lie is already compounded pretty well, isn't it?"

She sighed. "I know, I know. I didn't know this was going to happen. It was supposed to be so simple. Just a faraway husband—and no problems. I mean— everybody's a stranger to me here. It shouldn't have been a problem."

"Hmm. Do you know what happens if you go to the top of a hill, make a tiny snowball and start it rolling down?"

"Yes."

Jordan looked sideways at her. "That's an analogy," he explained.

She rolled her eyes. "Gee, I'd never have guessed."

"You have a big giant ball of snow heading toward you. The longer you keep it rolling, the bigger it will get. The bigger it gets, it's all the more difficult to ignore and impossible to hide."

"Let me worry about that."

"I think I may be a piece of gravel stuck in the snowball," Jordan mused. "Along for the ride and pretty much stuck there, but unable to do much about it so I might as well enjoy the view."

Hailey couldn't help snorting with laughter. "Analogies aren't your strong suit, are they?" she asked.

"Hey, I thought I was doing rather well, actually."

They pulled into Hailey's driveway and carted her belongings inside. "Thanks for your help," Hailey said, rubbing her palms on her jeans after depositing the last box—filled with teachers' manuals—on the living room floor. "I appreciate it. Everything. The drive and the carrying and..."

"The phone performance and the analogies?"

She smiled back at him, a bit uncertain. "Yes. Especially the phone performance. You're a good sport." She owed him something, didn't she? Of course, Mrs. Crumbs had already stuffed him full of home-cooking and dessert. "Would you like a beer? Coffee? Anything?"

Jordan folded his arms on his chest and looked at her with that amused half smile she thought she might be starting to hate because it tended to make her squirm.

He was the only one who knew her secret—and somehow that made him the only person in town she felt secure with, safe to talk to, not at risk of blurting out the wrong thing.

But he was *not* safe to be around—for totally different reasons.

"Yes, I want something. I want to understand your reasoning behind this thing."

"Didn't I already explain it?"

He looked down and seemed to be choosing his words carefully. "I understand your reasoning in theory—but I think you've chosen the wrong method."

Hailey threw up her hands in defeat. "Yes. You're probably right. I shouldn't have come here."

He looked up. "I'm glad you came here. But the whole Robby thing…" He shook his head. "You're digging ditches, burning bridges, all the big, bad clichés."

"It was necessary."

"Hailey, of course it's not necessary! Look, it really isn't that hard for a woman to hold men at bay."

"It is!"

"It's not! All you have to do is give us an icy glare."

"I don't give icy glares. And besides, then you—then *men*—just think I'm playing hard to get."

"Practice saying 'no thank you, I'm washing my hair that night' in front of a mirror." He shrugged. "You make it sound like you're having to fight men off. Frankly, I don't believe that can be such a huge problem."

"Thanks!"

He looked chagrined. "How do you always manage to make me say something unchivalrous?"

"I don't know. It seems to come naturally to you. Look—I'm not saying I'm Miss Universe and men are falling all over themselves around me."

He didn't object, and she continued, slightly disgruntled he hadn't tried to restore his reputation as a gentleman by saying Miss Universe wouldn't hold a candle to her. "If I let a guy close—and we're speaking relatively here—if I spend a lot of time around an available nice guy, next thing you know…"

"Practice no-thank-yous," he repeated. "If you don't want to see someone again, just say no."

"I hate turning guys down for such a simple thing as a date. It hurts their feelings."

"We're tough. We can take it. Hell, most of us are used to it."

"I can't. It's easier to go out with them at least once, and then I'm back in an evil cycle again."

"I see. And what it comes down to is that now you're living in Alaska, not to mention married to dear old Robby, because you don't want to hurt men's feelings?"

"No…"

"You're just being a drama queen and enjoying this whole farce?"

"No!"

"Then what?"

"This is safe! I don't have to…"

"That's right, Hailey. You don't have to fight yourself. The whole married facade is for yourself, isn't it? It gets you off the hook. It's there to provide you with an excuse—you're a respectable married school-teacher, you're not allowed to flirt with anyone, you won't have to turn anyone down because they won't ask—unless they're jerks who'd hit on a married woman anyway. Don't you see? You've manipulated things so that you're protected by the situation. This is not internal control, which is what you really want to achieve."

"Damn!" she yelled, swirling around to put her back to him. Her fists clenched in impotent anger. He was right and she hated it. She'd found a way to sneak around her problem instead of curing it. "Oh, damn," she muttered again, her anger fading. It wasn't his fault. She'd been lying to herself all along.

"Yes. Damn, indeed."

"You're right. I hate it when men are right."

"Okay, help me to understand the real problem. Why do you want this in the first place?"

"Why should I tell you anything? Besides, I already explained it to you. In the middle of a snowstorm, no less."

"This is what I understand. Your problem is that you have been unlucky in your relationships, so you want to take a whole year out, without any such entanglements, wipe the slate clean, so to speak. Start afresh, with no emotional baggage.''

''Correct.''

''Okay. And how exactly did you decide to bring Robby into this?''

''I didn't think it through,'' she answered reluctantly. ''It wasn't a *decision*. More like a knee-jerk response. Happened accidentally.''

''What do you mean, accidentally?''

She tugged at her hair. ''I mean, the first guy I met here...I thought I saw something in his eyes, and I panicked and blurted out that I was married. And after that—well, my fate was sealed.''

''The first guy you met... That was me, wasn't it?''

She just bet her face was well lit up now. ''Yes.''

''I looked like a male predator, did I?''

She folded her arms on her chest and bit her lip to keep the laughter away. This wasn't a laughing matter. She made sure she had her face under control before turning to face him. ''Well—telling you I was married seemed to make sense at the time.''

''That's a rather elaborate scheme just to get out of being asked out on dates. I repeat, ever heard of a little word called 'no'?''

''It's not that simple.''

''It *is* that simple, Hailey.''

She bit her lip—a nervous habit she'd been trying to break, especially since it was supposed to look extremely sexy to some guys. ''It *should* be that simple...but that's where my relationship addiction comes in.'' She held up a hand when he opened his mouth to answer. ''Don't say it! Just don't say it!''

"Why do you think you know what I'm about to say?"

"Too many talk shows? Too many self-help books?"

"No. I was going to say it sounded like you'd done too much thinking in circles, getting nowhere. I know that feeling. It's almost claustrophobic, isn't it?"

She shrugged. "Yes. Like there's no way out."

"Now that you've achieved some distance, are you still sure this is really a problem?"

"Of course it's a problem! I wouldn't have come all the way out here if it wasn't a problem, would I? I get too involved, too soon—and it damages every relationship I've ever had. Even with those who weren't jerks from the start."

"Okay. Too involved, too soon. Go on."

"I used to blame it on them. They were too superficial, too shallow...they weren't really interested in me... But then I read this book about taking responsibility for your own life." She raised her eyebrows, daring him to roll his eyes. "And it's me. My choices, my decisions, my expectations, my stupid belief in true love."

He raised an eyebrow. "Stupid belief in true love?"

"I don't know. The jury is still out, but love is quite possibly just a biological trick to get us to perpetuate the species," she muttered.

"Metaphysics aside, from where I'm standing, you don't have a problem. You've just been unlucky."

"Thank you, I feel so much better knowing it's all in my head."

"However—*we* have a problem."

His voice deepened, but she refused to notice. She

didn't know what he was talking about. She absolutely did not have a clue, and looked away from him for good measure, staring out the window into the backyard so she wouldn't see how the color of his eyes would have morphed from silver to the deep, intense color of storm clouds. "You mean the lie thing? That's *my* problem. Don't worry about it. I'm sorry I got you involved."

"That's not what I'm talking about."

"There is no other problem. *We* do not have a problem."

"Well, *I* have a problem."

She took a step back. It made her feel safer—sort of, although she wasn't sure if she wanted to flee him or herself. "Fine, fine. I think you are referring to…vibes. I already explained that. There are no vibes."

"Right. It's simply atmospheric disturbance. Solar storms—wasn't that what you said?"

"Yes. Exactly. Natural laws. Chemistry."

"Chemistry? Yes, can't argue with that."

"No!" This wasn't going well. "I mean, molecules and ions and all that. You know, like electricity makes the hair on your head stand up? Nothing to worry about."

"But—"

"And besides, I'm leaving," she rushed to interrupt him, terrified of where this conversation was going. "There's no point. With all the lies I'll never be able to return here even if I wanted to—and you're not leaving for the next decade at least. See? Not meant to be."

It was amazing how his eyes could look so winter gray and yet emit such heat. "It's a shame though."

"Yes," she'd admitted before she'd thought it through.

"In the right place at the right time…"

"The right time isn't in this lifetime so there's no use talking about it."

"We could do a chemistry experiment."

"No. Absolutely not. I'm opposed to chemistry experiments. Much too risky. I know kids who've blown up half the classroom."

"We're not kids. And we'll be careful."

Oh, God. He'd moved closer and he smelled so good she forgot all about safety gear and eye goggles.

"Jordan…" He was touching her hair, wrapping a strand around his finger. She shouldn't feel it. Hair wasn't alive. But she could swear she felt his rough fingers like they were on her skin.

"I never knew I had a weakness for blondes," he mused, letting go of the strand of hair. She didn't even manage to draw a breath of relief, before his hand dived deeper into her hair, cupping the back of her head, his thumb stroking her scalp. Goose bumps streaked down her back and up again, making her breath catch as she met his eyes. "But maybe I don't," he continued. "Maybe it's just you."

"This is not a good idea," she stammered. "Definitely, absolutely, positively not. In fact, it's a bad idea. A rotten idea."

"It's the best idea I've had all year."

"You know there's no point. It can't go anywhere. Too complicated…"

"We're not getting married," Jordan murmured.

Oh, God. He was kissing her jaw, close to her ear, his bristly cheek rubbing hers, and her goose bumps got goose bumps. ''We're just going to kiss.''

''We shouldn't.'' She was weakening. She could hear it in her own voice, and if she heard it, Jordan was hearing it too. Damn!

''Why not? What's the harm?''

''I was going to stay away from men! No dating! Remember? My resolution! The reason I came to Alaska in the first place! It's *important.*''

''We're not dating either, Hail.''

Hail. Had he just given her a nickname? A wintry, Alaskan kind of nickname. It was kind of sweet. She might want to keep it, even though she was pretty sure nobody could make it sound the same as Jordan did.

''What are we doing, then?''

''Nothing much—now.'' His arm came around her, crushing her against him. ''But any second now, we'll be kissing.''

She couldn't pull away. It was impossible. Just once would be okay, wouldn't it? Once didn't count. ''Okay…but just…once, right? Because, you know, once can be an accident. An experiment. But twice, and it's definitely equal to a date, and that will mean I've broken my rule. And I can't do that, because I have only two and a bit months to go, and I'm almost home clear.''

''You're cute when you're babbling.''

''How would you know? Your face is buried in my neck.''

''Your fault for smelling so good.''

''Jordan…you're driving me crazy, you know?''

''In a good way?''

She whimpered. "I don't know."

"Did you say once is okay? Just one kiss?" He was still speaking into her ear, the warmth of his body melting hers, but he wasn't kissing her yet. Damn. She reached for him, tentatively, wanting to hold as well as being held, her hands slipping up his chest, cradling his neck. She took a deep breath, pushing her nose hard into his sweater. Yummy.

"Yes," she confessed. "Once is okay. Then it must never happen again."

Jordan's warm rough hands covered hers, squeezed them before removing them from his shoulders, then kissing the back of each one before releasing her. He stepped back and put his hands in his pockets. "Terrific. I look forward to it."

"Huh?"

"We'll have to choose the time and place carefully."

"What?"

"Well, it stands to reason that if you're leaving in two months, and I'm only going to get one kiss, I'm going to make damn sure it's going to be a good one. That means careful preparation."

"Preparation?"

"Yes."

How could he be grinning when she was about to faint from disappointment? It wasn't fair. It wasn't gentlemanly. It wasn't *flattering*. "How exactly do you prepare for a kiss?"

"Meditation?"

She was off the hook. It wouldn't happen. He'd backed off.

That should be a good thing.

But it wasn't.

It wasn't good at all. "You're serious?" she almost yelled. "That's it? You go to all that trouble to seduce me and then you back off from the stupid kiss? You're going to leave me like this?"

"Like what?"

"All…" Hot and bothered? She felt like stomping her foot. She also felt like wrestling him to the floor and kissing him whether he liked it or not. "All *nervous!*"

Jordan looked rather pleased at this news. "Do I make you nervous?"

"Yes!" *Especially when you cheat me of a kiss!* There should be a law against this sort of thing. "You promised me a kiss, dammit, and I intend to collect! I want to get this over with."

"All in good time."

She took a deep breath and released it, vaguely surprised to see she wasn't exhaling fire. "That's pretty arrogant, you know."

"Mmm. And I make you…nervous."

"Yes!"

He grinned. "Excellent."

"What the hell is excellent about it?"

"You curse an awful lot for a schoolteacher."

"You bring it out in me," Hailey muttered.

He touched her hair, wrapped a strand around his fingers, then let go. "You make me nervous too, Hail."

"I do?"

"Yeah. All the more reason for careful planning."

"You don't *plan* kisses! They're supposed to be spontaneous!"

"Your fault. You're the one who insists there's only going to be one."

She pressed her still-tingling lips together and gave him one of those frosty looks he'd recommended. "Don't count on it, buster. All offers have an expiration date and this one does not have a long shelf life."

CHAPTER SEVEN

To: Ellen
From: Hailey@MySelfImposedExile.com
Things are getting worse!

Now Robby and I are having cybersex on a regular basis. And another guy promised to kiss me. Of course, it's not going to happen. I'm too busy spending my evenings naked in front of the computer writing sexy e-mails to my imaginary husband to actually kiss a real-life guy.

In short, life is also complicated out here.

Hailey

P.S. Yes. That guy. Stop squealing. It's not going to happen.

HAILEY enjoyed waking up in her own bed—well, Jane's bed—staring up at the ceiling, knowing she was relatively safe from random splashes of icy water from above. She lay for a while, thinking back on yesterday, then decided she was better off thinking about something else altogether.

Helena had been pleased to see her again—in a cat-like fashion. She'd jumped in the window as soon as Hailey opened it, but ignored her all evening. But as soon as Hailey had turned out the light, the kitten had sauntered into the bedroom and taken her customary place at the foot of the bed.

As soon as she opened the curtains someone was at her back door, banging away. Admittedly it was rather late—and it being a Saturday morning she suspected it was Simon. She liked to sleep in, especially on those long, dark weekend mornings, and Simon had probably been in the back playing with the dogs, waiting for light to come on in her window. He'd done that a few times before.

She opened the door, still in her pajamas, grinning as she realized she no longer fumbled for the non-existent security chain, and Helena shot out to Simon. The boy took her in his arms, and the two of them rubbed noses in their customary fashion.

"We're going sledding," Simon announced, his eyes bright with anticipation. "Up in the hills where we can get a real ride! Dad said you should dress warmly."

"*I* should dress warmly?"

"You need mittens and a hat, and warm socks and a scarf." Simon's face scrunched up as he thought. "And of course normal clothes too." He giggled. "You can't wear outdoor clothes and nothing else."

"That would be rather silly," Hailey agreed. "But I didn't know I was going sledding."

The boy didn't even blink. "Dad said so."

Really? "Simon—are you sure your Dad said I would come with you?"

The boy shuffled his feet and allowed Helena to jump down. She lifted her paws in utter disgust at the wetness of the snow, and then pranced inside. For a homeless stray, she was remarkably suspicious of the outside world. "He said if you come with us, you need to dress warmly…"

Hailey grinned. The scenario was pretty clear—Simon had asked if she could come with them, and his father had probably replied that she could if she wanted to. Somehow Simon had gotten that mixed up with his own instructions to dress warmly.

But what the heck? She'd never gone sledding before, and besides, this had to mean Simon had forgiven her for not being Jane.

"Sure. Sounds like fun." The boy's face lit up, and Hailey grinned inside. She'd really managed to win him over. No mean feat for the less pretty teacher. "When are you guys leaving?"

Simon pushed his jacket sleeve up and looked importantly at his watch, tilting his arm so she'd get a good look too. It looked new. "Noon. That's in...two hours. Isn't it?"

"Great. Knock again when you're ready to leave, okay?"

The kid smiled. "Okay. 'Bye!"

She closed the door and leaned against it, smiling. She wanted to go sledding—and she'd come here not only to escape from her old life, but to seek new challenges, try something new. There was no harm in it, was there? Not with an eight-year-old chaperone?

Besides, she could use the exercise.

"This better be worth it," she panted. Simon was far ahead of them, shooting up the hill with the energy of a marathon runner, pulling his bright green plastic sled. "Oh, my God, is there no end to this hill?"

Jordan was pulling their sled. It was made of wood, big enough for three, and probably very heavy. He didn't seem to be bothered by it, or by the fact that she was hanging on to his other hand. She'd never have made it up on her own—every now and then she was literally being dragged up the hill. So much for independence—but then climbing a mountain had never been an item on her independence agenda.

"It's more fun if we go all the way," Jordan said, pulling her along. He wasn't even breathing hard, and he was dragging that heavy sled *and* practically carrying her. What kind of a body was he hiding under all those winter clothes if he was in this good condition?

Extra ten minutes on the treadmill. Better not think about his body. Or teenage meanings to going "all the way." She had to be seriously depraved to be having the thoughts she was having. It was the addiction again. It had to be. It hadn't lost its grip on her yet.

This was good. This was a test of her character, and she would not fail.

"Did we have to do this on a *mountain?*" she wheezed.

"A mountain? This barely qualifies as a hill!"

"It's a mountain from where I'm stumbling along."

"Come on. Just a few more steps."

"This will be worth it? You promise?"

"Promise." He put his arm around her waist, pulling her forward. "Come on. If you give up now, Simon will tell your entire class. You'll never live it down."

"You're right," she muttered, forcing one foot in front of the other. Simon was already at the top, sitting there on his sled, head propped up on a hand in a perfect gesture of not-so-patiently waiting. "Maybe you should just wave him on. This is going to take a while.''

''It's fine. He'll learn patience. Besides, I think he wants to know if you'll be scared when you see how far it is down there, and how steep the hill is.''

Hailey made the mistake of looking back. ''I see your point.''

''Don't show that kid fear. He thrives on it. If he sees you're afraid, he'll feed you stories of broken bones and bloody noses.''

Uh-oh. ''Stories—or facts?''

He put his hands at the small of her back and pushed. ''On you go. Almost there.''

''I can't help but notice you didn't answer my question.''

''Don't worry. I'll take care of you. You're perfectly safe. Now—walk.''

I'll take care of you.

Why did these words carry such warmth and reassurance when she was well on her way to becoming an independent woman who did not need a man in her life? These words, the very essence of what her problem had been all along—that pathological need to have someone to take care of her.

No, she wasn't cured at all, was she?

Self-loathing gave her fresh energy and she managed to reach the top of the hill without any more support from Jordan. Simon only needed one nod from his father, and off he went down the hill, his laughter echoing back up to them.

''Wow…look at that view…'' she breathed. White. Everything was white. Still, she could see the contours of houses, cars, the shape of gardens and beyond them, white open spaces.

"Do you want to start a snowball rolling down and see what happens?"

She rolled her eyes. "No. I got the analogy the first time, thank you very much. I don't need a real-life demonstration."

Jordan put down the sled and sat down. "You want to be in front or behind?" he asked, looking up at her with a grin.

"I don't know. Which do you recommend?"

"Depends on what you want. You've got a better view in front, but then again you may not want to see the view."

"The hill is rather…steep, isn't it?" It had been steep enough when climbing up. It looked even steeper from up here. "Just how much speed will we get up to?"

"I don't know. Never measured."

"Will we break the sound barrier?"

Jordan laughed, breath puffing from his mouth and causing his eyes to do their nasty trick with her heart again.

"I don't know. Let's see. If we get down there, and a second later hear your terrified scream, we'll know we broke the sound barrier."

"My terrified scream?"

"You're scared, aren't you?"

"I'm not *scared*. I'm just being careful and sensible." Before she realized what she was doing, she'd bent down to adjust his loose scarf. He looked at her, startled, and she shrugged in embarrassment. "Sorry, it's the schoolteacher in me. I'm constantly helping someone with their mittens or tucking their scarves in so they don't hang themselves on the monkey bars.''

''Hey, I don't mind. Tuck me in any time.'' He held out a hand. ''Come on. I suggest you be in front. That way I can hold on to you. You just close your eyes if you don't want to see.''

Hold on to her. Mmm. It almost wiped out the imminent process of sliding down a hill at a million miles per hour in a vehicle, which not only had no seat belts—but no seats either.

''Okay,'' she said, maneuvering herself in front of him. ''Remember, you promised me I'd survive this. I'm going to be rather upset with you if I find myself chatting with St. Peter in a few minutes.''

''No problem. I always keep my promises.''

She considered snorting at the very idea of a man keeping his promises, but got distracted when his breath tickled her ear, the little of it not covered by either her cap or her scarf. Did his lips touch it? Either way, she was getting goose bumps again, and it wasn't from the cold.

Dammit.

Jordan wrapped one arm around her waist, pushing at the ground with his feet and his other arm. They teetered on the edge, but he held them back. ''Ready?''

She nodded, then squeaked a yes as she grabbed Jordan's arms tightly. Even as the sled started sliding down and then picked up speed, she felt safe. His long legs were around hers, anchoring her in place, and his arms were secure around her waist, holding on tight. If they fell off, at least they'd fall off together.

Then the world started zooming by. The pressure

pushed her back against him, and she heard him laughing in her ear as he worked one hand loose to wave at Simon, standing at the bottom of the hill waiting for them.

He was right. This beat Disneyland.

As the sled came to a stop, Simon came running, his bulky body in the snowsuit vibrating with excitement.

"Isn't it fun? Isn't it great?" he shouted. "See why I couldn't wait for the snow to get here?"

Hailey's heart was pounding, and not only from the exhilaration of the ride. She didn't move until Jordan's arms loosened around her waist.

"Wow."

"Yeah. No wonder kids slave up the hill for this kind of ride, huh?"

"Yeah. We need a lift up there."

Simon nodded energetically in agreement, but his father shook his head. "Nah. It's more fun if you have to work for it."

Simon rolled his eyes, telling her he'd heard that argument too many times before.

"Hey, it builds character," Jordan said.

"Half an hour for a couple of minutes' fun?" she asked. "Seems like a lot of character."

"Yeah, it is, isn't it?"

"Dad! Mrs. Rutherford! Make an angel with me!"

Mrs. Rutherford. She hated getting called that in front of Jordan. He always sent her this look of amused tolerance and there were times she didn't trust him to keep her secret at all.

Besides, he might not mind her lying to the entire town, but his son was a different matter. For one thing, what would his mom say when Simon told her she'd spent the day with him? She *really* hadn't thought this through.

Jordan grinned at her. "Ever made angels in the snow?"

"I told you, I've hardly even seen snow before. We've played in the schoolyard, but the snow immediately gets trodden down there. No room for angels in a schoolyard."

Simon was at her side, pulling at her hand. "You're bigger than me, and Dad's biggest." He pointed, ordering her in her place, and dragged his dad to her side. "See? We'll make three. Big, bigger, biggest. It'll be just like Goldilocks' angels!"

"I see you're not the only one in the family mixing up fairy tales," Hailey murmured to Jordan as Simon threw himself on his back and started pumping his arms and legs up and down. She allowed father and son to drag her down to their level, giggling at how silly she felt, flapping her arms and legs like a clumsy dodo bird, but it was fun, feeling the cold press against her back and seeing the almost cloudless sky above.

Their three angels were parallel—one bigger, one smaller, one smallest. The tips of their wings touched—that had been Simon's idea. Hailey stared at them, trying to imprint the image in her mind, wishing she had a camera. She longed to keep the memory, a souvenir of her time in Alaska, a souvenir of Jordan and Simon.

Souvenirs?

The thought was unsettling and she pushed it away. She still had a couple of months remaining. Of course it would be hard to leave her new friends—but it had also been hard to leave her old friends behind to come here. She'd survive.

When Jordan returned home Sunday evening after taking Simon to his mother's, the northern lights were putting on the most spectacular display he'd seen this year. He stood outside for a long while, just staring upward, then remembered he had a neighbor for whom this was something new.

He knocked on her door and waited for her to show her wary nose in the doorway. She tended to look at him warily, like she didn't quite trust him—and it had only increased lately.

She'd promised him one kiss before she left—in that case, it had to be a goodbye kiss. Anything else would just complicate things, either way. It might douse the fire between them, or it might ignite an even bigger flame—either way it was not a good idea.

So, goodbye kiss it would have to be. He just hoped she hadn't been serious about the expiration date.

"The sky is putting on a show for you," he told her when she finally opened the door, gesturing upward when she frowned in question. She stepped out on the porch and looked, and he heard her take a sharp breath.

Five minutes later she still hadn't said a word, but was starting to turn slightly blue.

"Hail, I think you should go put some more clothes on," he suggested. She didn't respond. Gently, he nudged her the few steps inside. "Warmer clothes, Hailey."

She craned her neck, straining past him to keep

looking up at the sky. "Wow. It's amazing. See all the different shades of color?"

He smiled indulgently. "Yes. That's why I came over to show you. Put some warm clothes on and you can go look all you want."

"What are you, my mother?"

"No." He shut the door on her view. "But I *am* a dad. I'm in practice. Sweater, scarf, gloves."

"Okay already," she grumbled, yanking a drawer open. "If it's all gone by the time I get outside, you'll never hear the end of it, you know."

"I'll take my chances."

Hailey pulled on a sweater, then another sweater and a third sweater. The first two he could understand, but the third one seemed like overkill. "I've bought a lot of sweaters," she explained when she caught him staring. She picked up a fourth sweater, contemplated it, then put it away with regretful movements. "And I'm not going to have any use for them in California. So I better use them up while I'm here."

"Interesting. Woolen socks, too. If your feet are cold, you're cold everywhere."

She giggled. "You're talking to me as if I were Simon."

"Sometimes you do seem to have as little common sense," he muttered. She let him get away with one sharp glare, probably thanks to the northern lights waiting for her outside.

"Woolen socks, three sweaters. I'm ready."

"Scarf." He grabbed one of several long scarves hanging from the top shelf and wrapped it carefully around her neck. Then he grabbed a woolen hat and pressed it down on her head, far enough to cover her

ears. She rolled her eyes and he shook his head.
"Don't even try it. I know you're going to stay out
there for ages. If you catch a cold, my son will need
a substitute teacher—and he hates substitute teachers."

"You're a devoted father," she told him.

"I am."

"But you're a vet. You should know that you don't
catch cold from *being* cold."

"Don't argue with a medical expert. Now, come out
in the backyard. There's a bench there somewhere under the snow. We can probably excavate it."

"You're coming with me?"

"Someone's got to make sure you're not found
there in the morning, frozen into a statue."

"Wow…" she whispered when they'd sat in the
backyard for about ten minutes. "See that shade of
blue-green over there?" She pointed to the east, and
he did his best to distinguish which shade she meant.
"I'd like a sweater in that exact color."

He burst out laughing. "Women!"

Hailey grinned sheepishly at him. "Men! They
don't appreciate the fine art of shopping. It must be a
genetic defect."

"Well, look up there." He pointed to the north,
where green shades seemed to chase each other across
the sky. "That's the color of your eyes."

"Oh," she said wistfully. "That's romantic." She
turned her head and narrowed her eyes. "You must
use that line with all the girls."

He hadn't. The northern lights had never reminded
him of a woman's eyes before. But she wouldn't want
to know that, would she? "No, unfortunately," he an-

swered flippantly. "It only works if they have green eyes."

She grinned at him, then turned her attention back to the sky. "It's unbelievable. I mean, I've read about the northern lights, I've seen pictures, but I never imagined how beautiful they would be." She moved closer, and although he knew it was an unconscious need to share the beauty of nature, he had to fight with himself not to put his arms around her and rest his head on top of hers. It was an intimacy he had no right to.

"Do you know why there are all the different colors?" Hailey asked.

"Of course I know," Jordan said with dignity.

"Yeah?"

"Yes."

"Well?"

"It's magic. Everyone knows that."

She laughed softly. "It's chemistry. The solar winds hit the chemicals in the atmosphere. Nitrogen causes red, oxygen causes green."

"Chemistry, huh?"

She looked at him and smiled, the green of her eyes just as radiant as the sky above them. "But I like your theory. Maybe chemistry is magic."

"Yeah," he agreed. "I think it may be magic."

CHAPTER EIGHT

HAILEY was shoveling snow with an unusual display of strength when Jordan got home from work Monday. When she saw him coming she strode to the fence, beckoning him to meet her. He was more than happy to.

"People are talking," she said without preamble. There was a hot flash of anger in her eyes, but also anxiety in the way she was biting at her lower lip. "People saw us in your car this weekend, and now they're talking."

He shrugged. "People always talk. It can't be helped."

"I'm a married woman!"

He raised an eyebrow, and she stared at him, a slow grin blooming on her face, then melting into full-blown laughter. "God! I meant to say that they all think I'm a married woman. I'm so entangled in this stupidity, I almost believe it myself."

"Of course," he said wryly. "With a husband like Robby, who wouldn't?"

"He is pretty wonderful, isn't he?" she agreed. "He gives the best back rubs, too."

"Whoa. I'm already in on the cybersex, but that's more than I want to know. Spare me the intimate details."

"I was just talking about innocent back rubs!"

"Uh-huh." He shook his head. "I know guys like

129

Robby. They may start out with innocent back rubs, just to reel you in, but they have indecent intentions.''

"He's my husband. It's his duty to have indecent intentions on a regular basis!"

"Lucky guy. He's becoming pretty real to you, isn't he?"

She shrugged. "I'm playing a role. I have to immerse myself in that role or it's never going to work."

"You're not going to fall in love with a fantasy guy, are you? That would be pretty stupid." *And you're not becoming jealous of a fantasy guy, are you?* he asked himself.

"I'm not going to fall in love, period," she snapped back. "Let alone with someone who doesn't exist."

"Even if he has indecent intentions and gives great back rubs?"

She grinned. "Even then. But anyway—I suppose it's not a good idea for people to see us together again."

"Why not? Let them talk. Who cares?"

"I'm leaving. You're remaining behind. You're the one who'll have rumors circling, that you had an affair with a married woman."

"I couldn't care less. I've dealt with gossip since the day Simon was born. I don't care."

"Your son might care. I'm his teacher. He could get hurt."

"My son will have to learn to distinguish truth from nasty gossip. He's a bright kid and I have every faith in his ability to do so. I will help him."

"But…"

"Do you seriously want me to tell him that he can't

go over to your place to play with Helena—because if I'm seen anywhere near you, people might talk?''

She sighed. "No. I don't know. I just want what's best for everyone.''

"Don't worry so much.''

"Simon's a great kid. I love having him around weekends. I would miss having snowball fights with the two of you.''

"We're neighbors. We're allowed to interact. In fact—want to go skiing with us next weekend?''

"Uh…skiing?''

"Yes. Now that you've gotten to know the slopes, skiing is up next.''

She was shaking her head quite fiercely. "No. I don't ski. I don't even water-ski. I don't know how, and I don't want to learn. No, thank you.''

"Why not?''

"Let's see—standing on two lengths of wood, holding on to two additional pieces of wood and pushing yourself off the top of a mountain—I don't know, Jordan, but somehow the idea is less than attractive to me. On a sled, at least you're sitting down!''

"You're such a city girl,'' he said affectionately. "Don't worry. We'll start with cross-country skiing. It's just like walking.''

"Good. I'll walk instead.''

He caught her by the belt loop at the back of her jeans when she intended to escape the conversation by walking away.

"You have to learn to ski. You don't have a choice.''

She tried again to step forward, but he held on tight and didn't let go until she'd turned around to face him.

"Really? I don't have a choice? How come, pray tell?"

"Do you know what day is coming up?"

"All sorts of days. Thanksgiving, Christmas, New Year's."

"Skiing Day."

"Skiing Day? What's Skiing Day?"

"It's sort of Alaska's national holiday."

"You're kidding me."

He didn't even blink. "It's a tradition. The whole town skis together. Your kids too, the whole school. You'll never live it down if you don't come with us— or if you show them you can't ski. The kids will lose all respect for you."

"They all ski?"

"Of course they do."

She gnawed at her lip. "I guess that means I have to learn."

"You're in luck. I know a great teacher."

"This is exhausting," she wheezed. "Why does it look so easy when you two do it?" She squinted and could make out Simon's small form—way ahead of them. "It seems you just glide along without any effort—so why am I killing myself here?"

"You're doing fine. Your technique isn't bad for a beginner. Your muscles aren't used to this kind of exertion, that's all."

"Am I going to have the will to live tomorrow?"

"Probably not."

She groaned. "Fine. Fine. I'll spend the evening in the bathtub with a soggy book. That's my cure for any kind of depression."

"What kind of book?"

"I'm working my way through Jane's library. It's pretty eclectic. Everything from serial-killer thrillers to children's fantasies."

He chuckled. "Yeah, Jane's a bookaholic. She orders online to save money, but then ends up spending just as much in the bookstore anyway. I've no idea how she gets through all those books."

There was a fondness in his voice that had her suspicious again. Was there something between those two after all?

"Do you two know each other well?"

He shrugged. "She's my neighbor and my son's teacher."

That wasn't much of an answer. But then it didn't matter much anyway, did it?

Simon came flying toward them, turning in a sharp circle to end up at Hailey's side. "Show-off," she told him affectionately. He grinned, so much like his father when he smiled.

"You're doing okay," he said graciously.

"Think I'll make it through Skiing Day?"

"Skiing Day?" Simon looked at her curiously. "What's that?"

Hailey's furious gaze told Jordan he was in more hot water over this tiny white lie than he'd anticipated. "We should have a Skiing Day," he told them both. "Maybe get the whole neighborhood together for a day. Wouldn't that be fun?"

The full effect of Hailey's bad mood didn't show until Simon had left. She was once again shoveling snow when he returned from driving Simon home—that

woman seemed to actually enjoy shoveling snow!—
and when she saw him step out of the car she threw
the shovel away and stomped into the house, slamming the door so hard it would probably be heard for
miles.

He winced as he opened the door to his own house,
wondering how to make this right. He pondered for
ages whether to go talk to her, and Helena was considerate enough to solve the problem when she jumped
in through a window he was quick to open when he
saw her run across the backyard. Perfect. He'd take
the cat over as a furry little shield.

Hailey yanked the door open even before he
knocked, shovel once more in hand.

"Don't tell me you're on your way to do more
shoveling?" he asked in dismay. She just glared at
him, then concentrated on the hallway mirror as she
swept her hair back in a ponytail and pulled a woolen
cap over her head. He tried a winning smile, but it had
no effect as she was refusing to even look at him. "I
brought Helena. I know she's not strictly your cat, but
she's used to sleeping at your place, so I thought she
should be here now that it's almost evening…"

"Thanks." She took the kitten out of his arms, allowing her to jump to the floor, and walked out the
door, leaving him inside. He pulled the door shut and
followed her. "You're shoveling snow in the backyard?"

"I like shoveling snow. I want to make a path to
the hot tub anyway."

"What's wrong?"

"There is no Skiing Day," she snarled at him.
"You lied to me."

"Yes. You're right. I did."

"Why?"

"Because I wanted to go skiing with you and you refused."

"Do you always lie to get what you want?"

He caught the undercurrent in her voice. "No. I don't lie just to be manipulative. This was only supposed to be an innocent joke. Hell—I didn't even expect you to believe it!"

"Just an innocent joke?"

"Of course. How could I have an evil agenda by asking you to ski with me? What's wrong?" Could that silly lie really have been so humiliating to her? "Why are you overreacting like that?"

"I've had enough of men lying to me, Jordan. I've had enough jerks lying to me just to get what they want."

Now *he* was a lying jerk? He took a deep breath. "Hailey, are you seriously yelling at me for telling one small lie, when I'm covering up for your whole life here in Alaska being one big lie?"

"That's not the same!" she shouted. "I lied because it was necessary and you should never have known! You lied because you wanted to get your own way, like a typical overbearing, selfish *man!*"

"Right. Robby is *necessary.* The bonsai trees are *necessary.* But telling a joke about Alaska having a National Skiing Day—which I never expected you to actually believe—is a capital offense. Great."

"Now I'm *stupid* for believing you? Wonderful! Now, just get the hell out of my yard and let me shovel snow in peace!"

"Fine!"

"Terrific!"

She was sniffing again. She probably had a cold. She couldn't be crying, because then he'd have to stay.

He stomped toward the fence, but one more sniffing sound, mingled in with the sound of furious shoveling, penetrated his anger, and his steps slowed. He turned around and was welcomed with a muttered curse and a microsecond of eye contact. She twisted away and strode toward the back porch.

She was overreacting. She knew she was overreacting, and he had every right to be angry at her for shouting at him, blaming him for one stupid tiny lie. And he shouldn't be following her. Why was he? Hysterical females were not fun to be around, and she hoped he wasn't coming back for another fight, because she was all out of angry adrenaline.

"Hey." He caught up with her and tried to touch her shoulder, but she twisted away and started shoveling, terrified to look into his eyes—not sure whether she was afraid he might see something in her eyes or vice versa. She wasn't up to another shouting match. She'd break down and start crying for real. "I'm sorry, Hailey. I shouldn't have shouted at you."

She didn't answer. A salty taste erupted in her mouth, and she didn't know quite where she was shoveling the snow to and from, but as long as she kept up this momentum, and her back to him, he wouldn't see the stupid trickling tears of meaningless self-pity.

She was *so* furious with herself.

"Hailey, talk to me!"

"Go away, Jordan." Voice almost steady.

Excellent. "I'm busy. I'll talk to you later, okay? When I've calmed down."

"I'm not leaving until we sort this out."

"There's nothing to sort out. You're sorry you shouted. I'm sorry I shouted. Very civilized. Now, please just go away."

"Hail..."

The nickname. It wasn't fair of him to use that on her. It always had her melting like snow in front of a fireplace. She kept attacking the snow, unaware that he'd moved around her until he said, "Dammit, you *are* crying!"

She covered her eyes with one arm. "I am not!"

"You are."

"Just go away. I'm overreacting. I'll recover. Just leave me alone."

"Skiing Day was just supposed to be a silly joke. I didn't think you'd take it like this."

"That's the trouble with men," Hailey snarled. "They don't *think*. Not with their brains, anyway."

Jordan sighed. "Don't do this again, Hailey! And don't lump us all together like that!"

She looked up at him, at his beautiful gray eyes, and swallowed. She wouldn't fall for him. She *wouldn't*. Even if that meant she had to lump him in with the rest of the jerks in the world. She yanked her arm out of his grasp. "I don't lump people together. I'm a teacher. I believe in individualism above all else, each person's individual character."

Jordan wasn't distracted. "I won't lie to you again."

"Don't make promises, Jordan."

"I mean it. I promise."

"I don't trust promises."

"Trust *me*." His hand was warm on her elbow again, and it was about the only part of her that was warm right now. "Trust me, Hailey?"

"I do. That was the problem. Get it? That was my *mistake*."

He hugged her, not a passionate embrace by any standard, but warm and caring and all those things she didn't want from him. "Come on. No more fighting. It isn't neighborly. Let's go back to my place. I'll make us some hot cocoa. Peace offering."

She sniffed, both tempted by the thought of hot chocolate in front of the fire, and feeling guilty and embarrassed at the way she'd reacted. "Marshmallows?"

"Of course." He took the shovel out of her hands and snagged it on the back door handle. "Lots and lots of marshmallows. You can't have hot cocoa without marshmallows."

"Is that the First Amendment of Alaska?"

He grinned, and flicked a tear off her cheek in such a casual movement that she almost didn't notice it. "No. Just my personal rule."

She got a black mug, filled with hot chocolate with dozens of tiny marshmallows floating on top.

"Feeling better?"

"Yep. And I'm not going to apologize for the hysteria. You should have walked away. When you didn't, you brought it on yourself."

"I can take a bit of hysteria, don't worry. I see neurotic animals all day long."

"I would take offense to that, if I didn't know that you like animals more than you like people."

"More than I like *some* people," he corrected.

"It's not a bad thing, really." Hailey mumbled. "I like Helena a lot better than some of the people who've passed through my life. Certainly better than most of the men." She shook her head. "Sorry. I keep sounding like a bitter old maid, don't I?"

"You've been unlucky."

"Maybe I was born under an unlucky star."

"There are no unlucky stars."

"No?"

"No." He stood up and held out a hand. "Come here."

She hesitated only a moment before taking his hand and allowing him to pull her to her feet. He headed toward the back door and stepped outside.

"My shoes are by the front door," she said, hesitating. "Where are we going?"

"Not far." He turned around and then she was in his arms, being held close to his chest as he strode through the snow into the middle of the backyard. Her arms went around his neck even as she decided this shouldn't be happening at all. She'd never been carried like this before. It felt far too good. "Jordan?" she squeaked. "What are you doing?"

Jordan tilted his head back, looking upward. "Look," he whispered. "Just look."

She followed his lead, staring upward at the millions of twinkling stars.

"Could any of these stars be unlucky?" he whispered.

Hailey tilted her head until it rested on his shoulder,

her arms tightening around his neck as she relaxed against him. Just for a moment, she told herself, before reluctantly raising her head again. No point in fighting to be put down though, she'd just sink a foot into the snow in her socks.

Jordan was no longer looking at the stars. He was looking at her and there were also stars in his eyes, no less bright and magical than the ones above, tiny pinpricks of warm light that seemed to penetrate through her. He was smiling, the small groove at the corner of his mouth speaking to her. She wanted to put her thumb in that groove. She wanted to feel the rasp of his stubble against her palm. She wanted to keep making him smile forever and ever.

Not good, she chided herself. No men, remember? No men. Not even a sexy Alaskan with the sparkle of winter stars in his eyes and a smile that melted icicles. Not even a man who believed in magic.

Not now.

Not ever. She wasn't staying in Alaska—and he would never leave.

His smile faltered. "What's wrong?"

What *wasn't* wrong? "Nothing's wrong. You're right, there are no unlucky stars." She cupped his face in her hand and, on an impulse she'd probably regret very soon, kissed his cheek before resting her head on his shoulder again. This was all very surreal. "You're sweet, Jordan. I should find a man like you back home." A frown appeared between his eyes and she shook her head to stop him from speaking. "Now, carry me back inside the house and put me down before even Aries and Orion start gossiping about us."

CHAPTER NINE

I SHOULD find a man like you back home.

Jordan bent over the sedated puppy on his surgery table, pushing thoughts of Hailey out of his mind while he finished the last stitches. Then as soon as he discarded the needle, Hailey popped right back into his head, practically smirking at him.

What was he going to do about her? Thanksgiving was coming up—and after that it would only be a few weeks until she was gone.

He stroked the puppy's head, murmuring something soothing before nodding to his assistant to finish up. He'd neutered the puppy. He wondered wryly—and with a wince—if the same method would solve *his* current problem.

He'd gotten involved, and it was damned annoying.

Her words had reminded him of what he'd somehow managed to repress lately, what he'd ignored while continuing to let their friendship blossom, tease her over Robby, take her sledding and skiing and offering her cocoa in his kitchen.

It wasn't meant to be. Now she'd confirmed it.

The first thought had been that this was good news: she wanted a man *like* him. The second thought had been that this was bad news—she didn't want *him.*

Of course, the bad news was really good news, since he didn't want her either. She was a temporary presence in his life—a temporary presence in this town.

He could not afford an emotional involvement with someone who was leaving—a woman who would tempt him away from his son. He didn't want to feel unhappy with the choice he'd made of staying as close to his son as he could throughout his entire childhood.

It was a choice he would never regret, but she was sure making him wish things could be...different.

Thanksgiving suddenly loomed—and Hailey was a bit lost. Going home for the holiday wasn't an option, not when it was only a few weeks before she would go back for good.

But to spend Thanksgiving alone, when she was used to having the extended family around her? Buy something called Zap-A-Turkey and eat it in front of the television? Even with Helena around, that would probably translate into a weekend of depression and self-pity.

She fielded a lot of "What are you doing for Thanksgiving?" questions at work, answering with a smile that she hadn't decided yet. But with only two days to go, that excuse wasn't convincing—and in the end Mrs. Crumbs took control of the situation. Hailey found herself back in the old lady's house, along with a horde of her children and grandchildren. There were also assorted other people who seemed to have no place else to go. Including Jordan.

The whole thing turned out to be a disaster.

"Do you have a name—or some kind of identification tag—for that oil rig?" one of the many daughters-in-law asked. "My brother once did some consultant work for a oil company, he might be familiar with it."

It went downhill from there.

"When I leave here," Hailey said with her jaw clenched as she sat in Jordan's passenger seat during the short drive back to their houses, "I never ever want to hear about oil rigs again. Never. That twelve-year-old managed to pull up pictures on the Internet and was asking me which one was my husband's."

"Lying is getting increasingly complicated in the information age, isn't it?"

"And Mrs. Crumbs keeps insisting Robby talk to her class over the phone or online."

"I see."

"What am I going to do?"

"Tell her it's impossible."

"Maybe I could get someone to pretend they're him," she said tiredly. "I already did it once, and it worked."

"Don't make this any worse than it already is."

"Any worse? I'm already having cybersex with the guy and I'm not even sure what cybersex is!" She squeezed her eyes shut. "And no, don't explain it to me. I don't want to know."

"You think I would know?" His tone was somewhere between amusement and indignation. "If anyone should explain it to you, it should probably be Mrs. Crumbs. She seems quite knowledgeable on the subject."

"Must be nice for you," Hailey muttered, annoyed at the laughter lacing his voice. "Your own personal soap opera, right next door."

Jordan parked in his garage and shut off the engine. "Where did you spend last Thanksgiving?"

"At home, with my parents and grandparents, and

brothers and nephew and nieces—and assorted friends and distant cousins.''

''A boyfriend?''

''No. We'd broken up by then.''

''Are you over him?''

''Are we doing girl-talk again?''

He chuckled. ''Nah. I'm just being nosy.''

''I'm over him. In fact, I think I'm over the whole thing now.'' She sighed, full stomach of delicious food making her drowsy, and now that she was away from all the people she was lying to, even content. ''Yes, it's been going pretty well, hasn't it? Despite Robby. Just one more month and I'll be free. Then we'll see if this experiment did me any good.''

''How are you going to test that?''

''There isn't a formal test. I'll just go back to my normal routine—and hopefully I'll have a new outlook on life.''

''What was wrong with the old one?''

''I told you—relationship addiction. Whenever I broke up with a guy, I was dating someone else within a couple of weeks. It was like I never felt complete, like a real person, on my own.''

''Complete?''

''I was *supposed* to be dating someone. That's what single women are supposed to be doing—looking for Mr. Perfect.'' She shrugged. ''Yeah, I know, this is the twenty-first century, things should be different. But they aren't.''

''There are no perfect men, so not much sense looking for them.''

She snorted as she opened the car door and climbed out. ''No perfect men? Wrong! Now there is Robby!''

* * *

The first thing Hailey did after saying goodbye to Jordan was decide to test out the hot tub on the back porch. Only a month to go—not a lot of opportunities left. She checked Jane's sticky notes for detailed instructions on how to work the—rather complex—tub system. It was pretty amazing that this thing even worked in winter, but Jane had assured her it wouldn't be any problem.

While the tub filled, she watched television and fielded phone calls from family. When the tub had finally filled it was getting rather late, but no point in wasting the water. She dug her swimsuit out of the suitcase—come to think of it, it had been rather optimistic of her to even pack one—and jumped in.

Wow. Tiny icicles really did form on her hair. Fascinating. The water could be warmer—it probably should be warmer, but the controls seemed to be stuck.

"Everything okay?" Jordan was at the fence, peering through the darkness at her. She squealed and sank under the water again, welcoming the warmth of the water on her icy shoulders.

"Hey. Yes, everything is fine. I'm testing out the hot tub. How about you? Doing a Peeping Tom?"

He rested his arms on top of the fence and chuckled. "Sorry, but since you weren't considerate enough to leave the porch light on I can't see a thing. I heard some noises, just checking if everything was okay."

"Everything's great. Except the water could be warmer. Hey, can you come over and help?"

"Wash your back?"

"No. The controls are stuck. You may not be able to budge them, but it's worth a try."

"Hail, am I hearing you correctly? Are you actually admitting I may be able to do something you can't?"

"You *are* stronger than I am. That's just biology. It doesn't count. Can you fix it or not?"

He climbed over the fence, opened the panel and fiddled around. "There."

"It worked?"

"Yeah. No problem." He turned back toward his house. "You'd probably already loosened it. Well, have fun."

"Wait—Jordan?" *No, no, no, no,* her conscience shrieked. *You're not about to do what I think you're about to do, are you?*

"Yes?"

She hesitated, and used the time to push her conscience down to the bottom of the pool and drown the annoying voice. "If I invite you in here with me—as a friendly neighborly Thanksgiving gesture—will you take that as a come-on?"

He grinned. "Yes. I would."

Good. Of course he was probably still *definitely not interested at all,* but nevertheless, good. "Fine." She laid her head back and looked at the stars. "In that case, you're not invited."

"Of course, if you were to specifically tell me it wasn't a come-on…"

"Would that work?"

"Maybe…"

"Maybe?"

"Yes. That would work."

"Okay. You can come in, if you want. If you don't think I'm trying to seduce you. And if you have trunks,'' she added as an afterthought. ''No skinny-dipping.''

Jordan was laughing again. ''Terrific. Be right back.''

He was back only moments later, but she'd still had the chance to regret her impulsive offer. Did she really want an almost-naked man in her tub? An almost-naked Jordan?

Yes—but she shouldn't. She still had over a month remaining of her no-men period, and she wouldn't allow Jordan to mess with her plans. It was bad enough that he made her want to.

Of course, it was a very stupid idea to spend a romantic evening under the stars in a hot tub with someone you were intent on keeping as a platonic friend. They were playing with fire—a neat trick in the water—and she knew it, knew it without feeling any inclination to back out. It would be easy. All she had to do was jump out of the tub, and into her robe, and tell him this wasn't a good idea after all.

Then he returned, running through the snow—barefoot!—wearing a dark blue robe with an intricate pattern of green and red that reminded her of something a fantasy wizard would wear, and she remembered how she kept wondering what his shoulders looked like under those scrumptious sweaters that he wore, and changed her mind again.

She definitely wanted him in here.

But just as definitely it was not a good idea.

Maybe she could look at this as a test. Even if he did make a pass at her, she would just say no. She'd practice an icy stare. She'd throw snow at him to cool him down.

But what if *she* made a pass?

Or had she already done so just by asking him in here? Even though she'd asked him on the understanding that it was not intended as such? Even though it probably was—she hadn't stopped to analyze her initial impulse yet—but she hadn't invited him in just for the company, had she? Not *really*. It was her hormones' fault. Had to be.

Why did everything have to be so complicated?

He sat on the edge of the tub, and grinned at her. Sometimes she hated how easily he read her mind. "Does that frown mean I'm no longer welcome?"

"I'm thinking about it."

"Anything I can do to aid the thinking process?"

Yes. Take your robe off. "No!" she yelled.

"Just asking."

"Sorry. Wasn't planning on shouting."

"Well? Am I in or out?"

"I'm not sure yet." She really should make up her mind. The man was barefoot and it was *cold*.

He trailed his fingers in the water, unfortunately at least a couple of feet away from all her body parts. "Are we playing with fire here, Hailey?"

Yes, he was definitely reading her mind. She sank deeper into the water, submerging her chin, feeling the water lap at her lower lip. "Well, we're playing in hot water, that's for sure."

He held her gaze for a moment. "And what's the verdict?"

She brought up her arm and let it fall again, intentionally splashing him as a response. "Get in. We're sentient beings. We can control our animal instincts— if we have those—even when out of our clothes.

We've decided nothing's going to happen—so nothing will happen. Nothing at all. Right?''

"Right."

"Good. Fine. So, come in here so we can get started on nothing happening."

"Okay," he said, and then she gulped and looked away like a shy teenager when he actually proceeded to do that. Seconds later he was submerged and she'd lost her chance to ogle. Damn.

"This is good for us," she told him, still staring in the opposite direction even after he'd eased into the tub. "We'll prove to ourselves that we can keep this platonic...despite these errant *vibes*. Right? It's a test, and we're going to pass. I *never* flunked a test in high school or college and I'm not flunking this one."

"Right," he said. His head was back and he was staring up into the sky, obviously having little trouble controlling his animal instincts.

Humph.

The water seemed much warmer after he was in it—and not only because he'd fixed the knobs. It was ridiculous to be so jittery. The tub was big enough for several people and he wasn't even close. No chance of even accidentally brushing against him. Double damn.

She saw the shadow of his legs moving under the water and felt uncomfortably hot. Maybe she'd see about cooling the water. Only, the tub controls were behind Jordan. In order to get to the controls, she'd have to straddle his lap, brace herself on his shoulder with one hand, while she reached over his head with her other hand...

Ever consider the possibility of just asking him to

move over? her annoying conscience sweetly asked. She slipped lower until the water covered her mouth, again hoping to drown out the irritating voice. Then Jordan moved slightly, causing a tiny tidal wave across the surface. Water slopped up her nose and made a valiant effort to reach her brain, causing an acute coughing session.

"You okay?" His hand was on her arm. *Not good, not good,* her conscience screamed, while the rest of her was rejoicing. "What happened?"

"Just swallowed some water." She coughed, feeling more stupid than ever before in her life. Drowning her conscience, indeed.

He let go of her arm and leaned back again. "Hail, not even you can drown in here."

"What do you mean, not even me?"

He looked significantly up at the roof.

"I was fine up there!" she protested. "It was just your arrogant machismo that insisted I wasn't!"

"Let's not fight, okay? It's Thanksgiving and we're not with our families—let's not start our own feud, here."

"Okay," she relented, but only because she didn't think she'd be able to keep her mind on all her logical fireproof arguments with him sitting practically naked a few feet away. Later.

"This is perfect," Jordan sighed, leaning his head back and staring up into the stars. Why was he so relaxed while her nerves were just getting more and more frazzled with each passing minute? "I've always meant to install a tub like this at my place."

"Simon would love that."

"Yeah, he would. He whines every once in a while.

I should get around to it before he's too old to enjoy it."

"I'm sure Jane would allow him to use this one once in a while."

"Probably. If we asked."

"What about you? Ever been in here before?"

Jeez, Hailey, you really do have a thing or two to learn about subtlety, don't you?

She wasn't sure if Jordan took her question at face value or not. He was still staring upward. "No," he said. "I don't make a habit of jumping into my neighbors' hot tubs."

Yes. That made her happy. Darn.

"Do you know the constellations?" Jordan was asking.

Hailey looked up at the canopy of stars. "No. Just the Big Dipper. Not even Orion. The kids tried to describe Orion to me, but I can never locate him."

Jordan pointed, steam rising off his arm, drops of water clinging to his skin and then raining into the water. "There he is. See, that's his belt."

Orion's belt wasn't very interesting. Jordan's chest was. She wanted to move into the cradle of his arms, lean back against his chest and look up with his cheek against hers. She wanted to brace her hands on his knees and feel the strength of his muscles under her hands. She wanted to feel his arms under the water, wrapping around her waist, and turn her head to look into his eyes, before he kissed her.

Whoa! Reality alert!

She blinked, and tried to concentrate on the stars. They looked foggy through the steam rising up from the tub. "Do you believe in astrology?"

"No. Humbug," he said succinctly, and she grinned, not surprised.

"Just wondering if you can see the signs of the zodiac up there."

"Probably. I have an astronomy atlas on my computer. I'll check for you tomorrow."

They soaked in silence for a long time, before Hailey noticed her fingertips were getting pruny. She'd always taken that as a hint from her body: let's get dry.

"Okay, I'm getting out. You can stay as long as you want."

"Probably smart to get out." He sounded drowsy. Not lustful at all, which was damn annoying. "Guess we shouldn't go to sleep in here."

She started to rise from the tub, but sank down again when he suddenly looked more awake. "Turn away," she commanded.

"Why? There's nothing to see."

"Nothing to see?"

He laughed. "I mean—you're practically wearing a full body suit."

"Nothing to see.... No wonder you're still single. Turn away until I'm in my robe."

"Aren't you used to parading around California's beaches wearing a bikini?"

"That's different." She wasn't sure *how* it was different, but it was. "Cover your eyes."

He made a face, then made a big show out of covering his face with his hands. "Prude."

She jumped out of the tub and struggled to push her wet arms through the arms of the terry robe without even drying off first. "Voyeur," she shot back.

"I didn't even peek between my fingers!" he protested. "Can I look now?"

"Yup. I'm going inside before my feet freeze to the porch."

"Nice toes!" he called as she hurried inside.

When she emerged from the bedroom, Jordan was out of the tub, lying on the sofa with the cat stretched out on his chest. His hair was still wet, sparkling with tiny drops of water, and he didn't even notice her. His eyes were closed, and she'd have thought he'd fallen asleep if his hand hadn't been moving over the cat.

The lucky feline was receiving long, slow strokes from the top of her head to the tip of the tail, and her purr vibrated through the room. Yeah, Hailey would purr too if she got that kind of treatment. His big, warm hand cupping her head, fingers running through her hair, warm, firm pressure of his hand sliding down her back all the way to the end of her tail...

Her eyes snapped open. *She did not have a tail.*

What she did have, she thought grumpily as she grabbed the cat, rudely waking Jordan up from his semi-slumber, was a severely dysfunctional fantasy life.

And she should not be fantasizing at all in the first place.

"What's wrong?" he asked, yawning.

"Everything," she answered, angry all of a sudden. Stupid fantasies would only lead to stupid mistakes, and what in the world had she been thinking, asking a man into the hot tub with her? "What the hell were we doing out there?"

"Nothing at all, more the pity."

"Yes. We shouldn't have. We shouldn't have been out there doing nothing! It was stupid!"

"We should have done something?"

"No!"

"You're not making much sense, Hail."

"Don't call me that!"

Jordan frowned. "Jeez. Sweet as an angel one minute, a hissing wildcat the next. You're a bit moody, aren't you?"

"Say the word PMS and you'll regret it," she warned him.

"Well, technically, that's not a word. Did someone put salt in your cocoa? What's the problem?"

"I'm leaving soon," she told him. "I'm leaving for good, we'll never see each other again."

"I know."

"Then what were you doing in my hot tub?"

"What's the big deal? You invited me, remember! You needed help with the stupid controls!"

"You're going to bring up the roof again, I just know it!" She clenched her muscles in an effort to keep herself from stomping her foot like a spoiled brat throwing a tantrum. "You are such a *man*."

"When did man turn into a bad word?"

"When they started lying and cheating as a part of their regular routine."

His voice turned dangerously soft. "Which one of us is living a lie, Hail?"

There was only one answer to that question, and she didn't like it one bit.

Two weeks later, after being relatively successful at avoiding Jordan altogether after that embarrassing disaster of a Thanksgiving, Helena seemed to be lost.

The cat who hated the outdoors had vanished...and didn't even respond to the sound of a can of tuna being opened on the back porch.

Hailey sighed and put on her boots and down jacket. She'd have to hunt the kitten down. But at least it was something to think about besides Jordan.

The backyard was littered with paw prints, and when she'd managed to find the ones that looked newest, she traced them to the back of the yard and into the forest. She sighed. Cats! Did Helena have enough brain in her tiny head to retrace her steps?

Or would she smell tuna if Hailey spread the contents of a few cans all over the backyard?

When that failed, there was only one alternative: trace the paw prints and see if she'd find her.

Hailey learned a lot about the lifestyle of the feline during the next half an hour. Helena had gone on a roundabout journey. She'd climbed trees, jumped into ditches, crawled under the roots of the trees and even, it looked like from the cat-shaped dents in the snow, taken nice chilly naps. Hailey was just about to give up and go home when she spotted the creature, far up a tree and looking as pathetic as a lost cat could.

Which was, not very.

"Helena!" she called. "Come on down here!"

To her surprise, the cat obeyed, rubbing itself against her boots and purring. Hungry. Definitely. Hailey picked her up and looked straight into green eyes. "Don't get lost in the forest, okay?" she chided. "I don't want to lose you."

Helena blinked and squirmed.

"You made me sick with worry, do you know that? And no, I'm not putting you down. We're going home and I'm carrying you!"

A snowflake landed on Helena's pink nose, and a tongue licked out to catch it. Hailey looked up to find the sky above the branches had turned dark. "Better hurry on home," she said to the cat. She stuffed the kitten into her jacket, leaving room for her head to peek out. Then she started retracing her steps.

The harder it snowed, the faster Hailey ran, but she wasn't quick enough. The footsteps vanished, and pretty soon she was wandering around, having lost all sense of direction. The sky got darker and darker— and having left her watch at home she couldn't even tell if it was just the weather, or if time had really passed and it was almost evening by now. Helena, sensing Hailey's increasing fear, grew restless within her jacket, but Hailey didn't dare put her down. Visibility was so bad now she'd lose the cat if she wandered just a few feet away.

She tried to calm the kitten down, and eventually Helena huddled down inside her jacket and was quiet.

But soon Hailey had to admit she was lost. All the trees looked at once alien and familiar, and she had no idea if she was walking in circles, on the way back home or in an opposite direction.

"You can't get lost," she chanted to herself. "You're practically in your own backyard for God's sake. Nobody gets lost in their own backyard! There's probably a law against it!"

But the words echoed hollow as her feet got weary, and walking seemed pointless when it brought her nowhere. She could no longer feel her toes, even inside the heavy winter boots.

Finally she slid down in the shelter of a big tree, in the nest between two overgrown roots. At least she was out of the wind. "We'll wait a bit," she whispered to the cat. "As soon as the storm quiets down, we'll find our way home. Don't worry. Nobody croaks from cold in their own backyard. I'm sure of that."

"Come on, guys!" Jordan whistled for Sam and Daisy, wanting them inside, but they seemed intent on having a little walk today. Both of them hung around the edge of the property, barking. He sighed as he put on a thick sweater, wrapped a scarf around his neck and pulled on his parka. "Fine, fine," he mumbled. "You run my life anyway, so of course I'll walk you even in a snowstorm."

He strolled toward the dogs, and nodded, giving them permission to leave the yard. They sprinted away immediately—and there was something in their bark that alerted him to possible trouble. He glanced at Hailey's house out of habit, and noticed there was no light in the windows.

She *should* be home. She was always home this time of the day. Admittedly he'd hardly seen her at all over the last couple of weeks—she was doing a great job at avoiding him. It wasn't any of his business where she spent her day, but...could there be something wrong?

A few more steps, and he could see the faint trail through her backyard, and a dip in the snow resting on top of the fence, where someone had climbed over it.

Could his city girl have gotten lost right outside her own backyard?

Fear already pulsing in his blood, he ran into the forest after the dogs.

Daisy and Sam found her immediately.

She was sitting under a tree, the snow piled high around her. Her arms were around her knees, her head down, and she didn't even seem to notice the dogs. He knelt down beside her, cupping her face in his hands. "Hailey!"

Her face was icy, her eyes glazed, but she helped when he pulled her to her feet. Not unconscious.

Too damn long since he'd seen her.

Something moved under Hailey's parka, startling him. Of course. The cat. She'd gone out here to rescue the kitten. Typical. He couldn't even blame her for that—he'd have done the same thing himself, but she should have come to him, asked him for help. This could end badly. His heart pounded against his ribs as he ran his hands over her, tucking in her clothes as if that would help, ripping off his own scarf and wrapping it around her face and neck. If she had frostbite or hypothermia…

Why did she have to be so stubborn and independent?

She still wasn't speaking. "Hailey? Are you okay? Talk to me."

She was staring at him as if he were a hallucination she didn't quite trust. Only semiconscious? He curbed his panic and looked at her carefully, checking her condition as objectively as he could.

Her face was pale, but there was not the deathly color of frostbite, and her lips were moving although she wasn't speaking yet. Relief blossomed. She was probably okay. She was shocked, afraid—but hypothermia had not set in. He'd get her home, into a warm bath, and she'd be fine.

She had probably decided to leave Alaska tomorrow and never leave California's beaches again, but she'd be fine.

"Jordan…" she whispered, and without meaning to, he kissed her, finding her lips cold, but not freezing. He pressed his cheek against hers, trying to warm her any way he could.

"Hailey—you're okay. The dogs found you. You'll be fine."

"What time is it?"

"Around five."

Now she started shivering, her teeth chattering as she spoke. "Two hours? I've only been out here two hours? It felt like ages. I thought I'd die." She gasped, looking around. "Helena! Where's Helena?" Her hands came around to her front, cupping her stomach almost as if she were pregnant. "She's here," she whispered. "She's fine. She's moving."

"Neither one of you is dying. Not with two canine noses on your trail. Besides, I wouldn't let you." He put an arm beneath her knees and whisked her off her feet before she could even think to protest. "Come on, let's go home."

"Jordan, I can walk, no problem, if you just point me in the right direction. I'm okay." She struggled to get down, but he held on tight, carrying her toward home, and didn't answer.

"Macho," she muttered, but slid her arms around his neck, anyway, resting her head against his shoulder. Fine. Five minutes ago she was sure she'd spend the rest of eternity as a skeleton sitting under a tree. She could tolerate machismo for a few minutes, and he was damn good at this carrying thing. Before Alaska, when was the last time someone carried her? When she was five? "Nobody carries women around anymore except in old movies, you know."

"Call me Gary Cooper," he muttered.

"I'm sorry when I said we'd never see each other again, like I didn't care at all..." She buried her face deeper in his shoulder, because she was close to hysterical sobbing, now that it was over and she was safe. "I'm sorry..." she hiccupped. "Please, ignore everything I say for a while. I'm not myself."

He didn't take her home, but next door, to his home. She didn't object—after the scare in the forest she could use the company. He didn't put her down until they were in his bathroom. He ripped off her gloves and boots, then her socks, his hands hot on her icy feet. "No frostbite," he muttered. "You'll be fine." He turned the taps, dumped a heap of towels on the counter and curtly ordered her to get warmed up.

Hailey took a warm bath, slowly adding more hot water until the heat started to burn the lingering chill from her bones. When she finally got out, Jordan was in the kitchen making grilled cheese sandwiches, and she sat down at the table, swathed in his robe. Her clothes had turned out to be both wet and cold, and she hadn't wanted to wear them again. "Sorry for the hysterics," she apologized with an embarrassed grin. "I don't know what came over me."

"Getting lost in a snowstorm is not fun," Jordan said. He put a plate in front of her. "But no harm done. Another hour or two, though, and you might have been in trouble. Eat.''

She dug in, still embarrassed. ''So, like how far away was I? Three feet from my fence?''

''Probably something like five hundred feet.''

She groaned. ''I feel so stupid. I didn't have any idea which direction I was supposed to go in.''

''Of course not. You're out of your element here. It's my fault. I should have taught you the basics.''

''I'm not your responsibility,'' she told him, then slumped over her food again, too tired and shocked to keep up her independent act. ''I know I'm supposed to be able to tell direction by checking the moss on the trees or something—but I wasn't sure what I was looking for, and if there's moss it's all covered with snow and ice...'' She was gibbering, wasn't she?

''Eat up. I'll light the fire so you can keep warm.''

Hailey finished her sandwich quickly, then she started to tremble again as she looked out the window into the raging storm. If the dogs hadn't sensed something...if Jordan hadn't listened to them...

Shivering more and more, she wrapped the robe securely around herself and fled the kitchen in search of Jordan.

He was in the living room, crouched in front of the fireplace, adding wood to the fire. She walked over to him and put her hand on his shoulder. His warmth penetrated through the sweater, into her palm, and shot up her arm.

She *needed* him.

''Jordan...''

He looked up and smiled. ''It'll be warmer soon.''

She sank to her knees at his side, looping her arms around his neck. "It's warm enough. *You're* warm enough."

Surprise flashed in his eyes, then doubt, as she squirmed closer, pressing herself against him. He started speaking, but she silenced him with a palm against his mouth. "Don't talk. Magic, okay?"

As soon as she'd breached his initial defenses and touched her lips to his, his kiss was sudden, and it wasn't gentle, wasn't soft or tender, it was heated and harsh and as relentless as the hands soon tearing at the belt of her robe. *Yes,* she thought with pleasure, *this is right, it has to be right,* frantically pushing at his sweater, desperate to feel his skin against hers.

But then all of a sudden he wasn't there anymore, and her robe had been moved back in place, the sash securely tied. And Jordan was standing by the window with his back turned to her.

She cleared her throat and tried to pick up the shreds of her dignity. "What now? Are you going to give me some line about not knowing what I'm doing because I'm in shock and you're too noble to take advantage of me?"

"Something like that."

"Terrific."

"I wouldn't go that far."

"Why are you being noble?"

"This year is obviously important to you, Hailey. Look at all you've done to keep that promise to yourself. I don't want to risk...us...over this."

"There is no *us!*"

"Oh. I see. This was nothing?"

"Yes. Nothing. I was in shock—I almost died out

there…I was just…'' She floundered, eyes swimming in tears now. ''You just saved my life…''

''Great! A roll in the hay as a thank-you for saving your life?''

''That was not a roll in the hay!''

''Call it what you want, lady, I was the one who stopped it from turning into—''

She covered her ears with her hands, not wanting to hear him turn those magical moments into something insignificant.

''There is no us,'' she repeated. ''There can be no us. I told you so from the beginning. Hell, I told you I was married just to make sure! I'm leaving and I'm never coming back—that's the fact.''

''And that's what you *want,* Hailey?''

His eyes were flashing anger, and she hoped hers were shooting furious sparks right back. ''Right. That was the goodbye kiss we were owed. I'm leaving soon and we'll never see each other again and that's exactly how it should be. Goodbye!''

''Excellent.'' He whistled for his dogs and marched toward the front door. ''We're taking a walk. Let yourself out whenever you're ready.''

''You're taking a *walk?*''

''Goodbye, Hailey.''

CHAPTER TEN

IT WAS time to leave.

She'd said goodbye to her students and her fellow teachers and returned her borrowed skis to Mrs. Crumbs' attic. The house was cleaned—all she had to do was pack her things—she'd even left the occasional sticky note in a strategic place, notifying Jane of this and that. Mrs. Crumbs had insisted on helping her get the house ready, and she'd refused to listen to Hailey's protests.

"Here you go, dear." Mrs. Crumbs handed her two colorful packages, displaying sparkling Christmas trees. "One for you and one for your Robby."

"For Robby…?"

"You can open yours now. I'd love to see if it fits."

Hailey tore open the paper to find a woolen sweater knitted in a delicate pattern. She took one look and knew she'd treasure it more than all the cashmere in the world. Sweaters knitted by arthritic hands were the most precious of all.

But…*Robby's sweater…!*

She couldn't do this anymore. "Hyacinth, about Robby—"

"His matches yours, but the colors are slightly different. More masculine. And the size, goes without saying, I hope it fits him."

"Oh, Hyacinth…"

Mrs. Crumbs waved away her thanks, and Hailey's

resolve to come clean wavered, then disintegrated. No use. She'd just leave Hyacinth disappointed and angry. "You may not have much use for yours back in California, but at least Robby can use his when he's on the rig. I bet it gets even colder in Siberia than it does here."

Dammit, dammit, dammit! "Hyacinth, this is so sweet of you." Hailey almost choked on her words, all the lies stealing her oxygen.

"You're welcome. Do me a favor, dear—I've grown quite fond of you—would you send me a picture of the two of you wearing your sweaters? Just a casual snapshot—you could e-mail it to me."

Oh, God!

"Of course," she said. It was the only thing she could say, although "Hyacinth, I'm a liar and a fake and Robby doesn't exist," was a close second. But that would be to assuage her own guilt—it would only hurt the old lady. "Of course I'll send you a picture." Somehow. Maybe. Saying "no" was not an option, of course.

They hugged, exchanging promises about keeping in touch, then Mrs. Crumbs left. Hailey clenched her teeth and strode upstairs to the bedroom to start packing.

Instead she curled up on the bed for a cleansing sob session before gritting her teeth and starting to pack— starting with a precious parcel of goodbye drawings from the kids.

She hadn't intended to say goodbye to Jordan—but there was Helena to discuss. She couldn't just kidnap the cat. She'd have to persuade him to let her go.

After piling her suitcases in the street and calling a

taxi, she took Helena into her arms and walked next door. She took a deep breath before she knocked. The dogs barked, and then Jordan opened the door.

"Hi."

"Hi."

"I'm leaving now, but there's one last thing we need to discuss."

He looked wary. Wary, and still angry. "Yeah?"

"The cat…"

"Helena? What about her?"

"She's going with me." Her tone straddled the line between a statement and a question mark.

"With you? To California?"

"Yes."

"No. She's not."

"Yes. She belongs with me."

"Why? This is her home. Alaska is her home."

"She's *my* cat."

"She's not *your* cat. Before you got here, she was nobody's cat, but for the last few months, she's been *our* cat."

"Well, we'll be living several states—and one large country—apart."

Jordan shook his head. "Are we having a custody dispute over the cat?"

"Looks like it."

"This is her home. She knows the environment, the climate. She's an outdoor cat. You can't keep her in a city apartment!"

"Animals adapt. Just like people adapt. Just like I adapted. And it's not like she's all that eager to be outside, anyway."

"Why should she have to adapt to something so different?"

"I love her."

"So does my son."

That was the hard part about this and it brought tears to her eyes. "I know. I don't *like* taking her away from Simon. But Simon already assumes she's going with me. He already said goodbye to her and everything."

"*What?* You told my kid you'd be taking the cat?"

"No! The last time he was here, he brought it up. Otherwise I wouldn't have dreamed of taking her. He thinks of her as my cat. He assumed I would be taking her with me. He said he'd miss her, but he understood that she needed to be with me and sleep in my bed." She heard her voice lose momentum and lower to a whisper. "Simon will be fine. He has the dogs and all the other animals you bring home. I only have Helena. I don't want to lose her."

He looked down for a long time, staring at the floor. Then he shook his head, shrugging. "Okay. You can have her. On one condition."

"What's that?"

He looked up at her—still looking angry, so at first she didn't quite comprehend his words. "You bring her back for a visit next year."

"A visit?" she asked carefully. "What do you mean, a visit?"

"Yes. The two of you visit us. Just once. Spring break or summer holiday—you bring her back for a visit."

He was so serious. So rarely had she seen him without the hint of a smile, in his eyes if not his lips.

"Why…?" she asked, almost afraid of the answer. "For Simon? Why?"

"Because." His lips thinned, a move similar to Simon's when that was all the answer she was going to get. Her mind struggled to make sense of what was happening—why he was asking this, and what it meant.

It could mean he cared. He was angry, but he cared.

Even though she did not want him to care, he did. That was the clincher. She nodded. "Okay. Deal." She gestured toward her house, where her luggage was heaped outside, desperate to lighten the mood. Fat chance. "I bought a brand-new cat carrier."

"She's never been in one before, has she?" he asked, eyeing the box dubiously.

"No. But there's no other way. Can you look at the box? See if she'll be okay in there?"

"Sure."

They walked over, and Jordan inspected the box, proclaiming it safe. "'Bye, cat," he said, giving Helena one last scratch on her belly before allowing her to peek curiously into the carrier, only to be deeply offended when Hailey shut the hatch on her.

"Will this traumatize her?" she asked, feeling horrible when the cat starting whining pathetically.

"Nah. Not for such a short time. Just pay her plenty of attention and make sure she knows you're there."

"Okay." She glanced up the street to find her taxi cruising toward them. "That's my ride. Well— 'Bye then, I guess. It's been…nice. Thank you for allowing me to take Helena."

His smile was tight. "'Bye, Hail."

There was more to say. She just couldn't figure out

what. She couldn't find any words at all, and they'd already said goodbye and he was just standing there, not speaking. And when he greeted the cabbie and started loading her luggage into the trunk, she grabbed the cat carrier and fled into the cab without another glance at him.

The cabbie chatted all the way to the airport, but Hailey didn't hear much of it. She was staring at Helena through the plastic grate of the carrier. She had promised to bring Helena back for a visit. She'd essentially promised to come back.

Did she have the right to make such a promise?

It had been a mistake. It was almost a commitment on her part, a commitment she couldn't possibly honor. She couldn't come back with all the lies between her and the rest of the town—a whole play she'd staged, a person she'd created.

No. She could never come back.

Jordan stared out the window, up at the sky.

The evening sky was clear, all the stars were out. Hailey would have a wonderful view from the plane, he thought, the lights below and the stars above—at least until she disappeared into her beloved smog back home.

He missed her already. She'd avoided him recently—they'd avoided each other with the imminent parting ahead—but knowing of her presence next door had been soothing.

Sam and Daisy sensed his mood, and theirs matched it. They whined, and depression leaked from their faces as they lay on the floor, heads resting on their paws, staring at him with the saddest eyes in Alaska.

He patted the cushion next to him, inviting them to join him, but even that didn't interest them. Were they blaming him for this?

"Broken heart, guys?" he asked them heavily. "Is that what this is? We'll get over it. Okay? And she promised to come visit us next year. I'm not sure she'll keep the promise—I'm not sure if she'll even remember us when she gets back to her old life, but you never know…"

He tilted his head back and closed his eyes, hoping he'd fall asleep. He didn't want to stay awake, one eye on the clock, just because a masochistic part of himself needed to know the exact moment when Hailey's plane lifted off and took her away from him.

The doorbell rang, and he opened his eyes, blinking. He glanced at the clock, and saw he'd dozed off for a while.

The bell chimed again. He contemplated not answering. His car was outside, but everybody knew he was frequently away on his skis, and there were no lights on in the house.

The dogs solved the dilemma, jumping to the door and barking. He had to answer. It could be someone with an animal in need of attention. With a huge sigh he pushed himself out of the chair and answered the door.

What waited there weakened his knees, almost causing him to fall.

"Hailey?" She was standing there, the cat carrier in her arms. She was real, and she was *here.* Not on a plane on the way to California. He reached out and touched her hair, just to make sure she wasn't a mirage. "Hail?"

Her eyes shimmered with tears. "I can't take her, Jordan. I can't." She thrust the box at him. "Here. Let her out. She'll be happier here anyway. It's for the best."

"What? Hailey, what happened?"

She was sniffing. "I'm going to miss my plane." But before he could react she added, "There's another plane I can take. But I had to return Helena. I can't take her with me…"

"What?"

"I can't take the cat with me—don't you see? I can't promise to come back."

He braced an arm against the door post, praying she wasn't saying what she appeared to be saying. He'd hoped, dammit—she'd missed her plane just to return the cat she'd fought for? "Why?"

She continued pushing the cat's box into his chest until he took it. It was heavier than he expected, pulling at his arms until he put it down, absently flicking the hatch open for Helena to escape. She sprang directly to Hailey, rubbing against her legs, purring as if to say she was forgiven for the imprisonment.

Hailey was talking fast, almost babbling, her eyes bright with unshed tears. "It's like a commitment, isn't it? Taking the cat, promising to bring her back…promising to come back after my year is over and I'm free…I can't do that." She shook her head in emphasis. "I can't promise I'll ever come back to Alaska." She looked into his eyes briefly. "I won't come back. Too many complications—too many lies."

"Wait." He grabbed her wrist, straining to make his touch light. "What are you saying?" Stupid question, he berated himself. She was being very clear, and the words had gouged his heart. Did he really want to hear more?

"I'm not coming back. I'm never coming back. I'm sorry." She nimbly pulled her hand out of his grasp. "I'm sorry. I have to run, now, or I'll miss my plane—again. Goodbye, Jordan."

"You're never coming back?"

She shook her head. She was pale and drawn, unable to meet his eyes more than few seconds at a time. "I can't come back…"

"I see," Jordan said. It was all he could say. He didn't have a right to that emotion—but betrayal was what he was feeling. "Goodbye then, Hailey. Remember the northern lights." He laughed—a short, bitter sound. "Magic, right?"

She stared into his eyes, then her gaze shifted to the cat, still circling their ankles. "Goodbye, Helena," she whispered. "I love you."

The sense of disappointment and loss was acute, much worse than when they'd said goodbye before. This was final. He stared after the taxi until it had vanished, but still furious with himself for not going into the house and turning on the sports channel or something, anything to just put this behind him and forget all about her.

It had been stupid to expect she'd come back.

Helena meowed at him, head-butting her former cage, pushing at the hatch with a paw. He stared down at her and remembered Hailey's last words. *I love you*—to the cat.

The searing feelings were impossible to ignore, bringing home a truth he'd been refusing to face.

He'd wanted her to say those words to *him*.

* * *

This had been the worst Christmas ever.

She'd always loved Christmas. Even after the excitement of childhood Christmas had worn off, she'd loved the Christmas preparations, the decorations, lights, candles, the music. She loved the tension in the air, the smell of a fresh Christmas tree—even the crowds in the malls.

But none of it was any good now. She missed Helena. She missed the kids in her class. She missed Christmassy snow. She missed a clear night sky filled with iridescent lights and billions of stars.

She missed magic.

Okay. The truth was she missed Jordan, and no matter how hard she tried, denial and repression weren't working very well. She'd considered calling him, wondering if the sound of his voice would make her feel better, if they could somehow establish over the phone lines that this was for the best—that they were back in their respective lives, worlds apart, and everything was exactly how it should be.

She'd also written e-mails, cheerful, depressed, defensive—even honest—but the delete button had always received a good workout in the end. Clean break. It was the only way.

"You can always go back, you know," Ellen told her, taking her arm and pulling her into yet another fashion store. "You should go back."

"I can't."

Ellen grabbed a pair of orange pants and held them against herself. The color reminded Hailey of Helena. "You *won't.* Big difference. And if you're going to continue moping around like this, without even a token interest in shopping, I'm going to put you on a plane myself.''

"I'm not moping.''

"What do you think about these pants? Isn't the color divine?''

"I thought we were going grocery shopping.''

"Are you telling me we can't shop for clothes at the same time? Is there *ever* a wrong time to shop for clothes? Did you get a lobotomy up there?''

"Never mind. That's a beautiful color. Especially in fur.''

"Fur?"

"Never mind.''

"After the new year, Hailey. Your year will be up. Go back and talk to the guy. Clear the air. You need to. You know you left a lot of unfinished business up there.''

"What makes you think he'll even want to see me?''

"I don't know. The way you've been acting since you got back, I'm not sure *I* want to see you. Are you coming with me to that party on New Year's Eve?''

"I suppose,'' she answered reluctantly. She wasn't in the mood for a party, but it was probably better for her mental health than moping around her apartment.

"You might meet a hot guy after midnight. In fact, you're destined to meet a hot guy after midnight. A year away from the action and you're owed some.''

"I'm not interested in action or hot guys, thank you. I just want this year over with and the new one to start.''

"It's been a year and you're *not interested?*

Obviously, you're cured of that imaginary relationship addiction.''

''Yup,'' Hailey sighed. Mission accomplished. It should feel better. ''I think I am.''

The party was a typical one, loud, crowded and filled with modern mating rituals. Hailey watched, detached, almost analyzing the moves. This was rather fascinating. Funny how she'd never noticed the details back when she was a part of the game.

It had worked, she thought with savage satisfaction. She wasn't feeling desperate to find someone to talk to, someone to dance with, wasn't measuring every guy she talked to as possible boyfriend material.

Then of course, she wasn't doing an awful lot of talking, as everyone seemed to migrate away from her after just a few minutes. She wasn't sure why until Ellen came swooping down at her, grabbing her arm and pulling her to the side. ''What the hell are you doing?''

Hailey held up her champagne glass. ''Partying!''

''You're releasing reverse pheromones.''

''Excuse me?''

''Reverse pheromones!'' Ellen shouted into her ear. ''Give the guys a break! Someone asked me if you were recently widowed or something.''

''Huh? Widowed? Why would anyone think I was a *widow?*''

''I don't know what you're doing, but stop it, will you! Or you'll end up as a spinster for good!''

Ellen's cell phone beeped, the sound almost drowning in the noise of the party. She yanked it out of her purse and brought it to her ear. "Hi. Okay. Just a moment."

The phone went back into her purse and she grabbed Hailey's wrist. "Come on. I need fresh air."

Hailey allowed herself to be dragged through the crowd, down the stairs and out the front door. Then the door slammed shut behind her, and she realized Ellen was on the wrong side of it.

"Ellen?" she called, banging on the door with the heel of her hand. "What the hell are you doing?"

"Matchmaking." A dry masculine voice came from behind. "I know now what you mean about your horrible matchmaking friends."

She almost didn't recognize him, his clothing was so different. She took a few steps closer before she dared address him. But it was him. His eyes, his mouth smiling at her. "Jordan?"

"Yeah. It's me." His eyes were drinking her in and she was sure she was doing the same. God, how she'd missed him.

"What are you doing here?" She was still wondering if she could be hallucinating.

"Your friend called me. Or rather, she called your old number, got my number from Jane and then called me."

"*What?* She got you to come here?"

"She asked me if I was going to be as stupid about this as you were being."

"Oh, damn."

"I told her it was your decision and she said, 'Yeah, whatever, write this down, here's where she'll be on New Year's Eve, just in case you come to your senses.'"

"If you're here just because Ellen told you I was moping..."

"No. She was right. We were being stupid."

"So why are you here?"

"I'm here because the rules change at midnight. And I didn't like the old rules one bit."

She glanced at the clock. It wasn't even close to midnight yet. Damn.

"I'm not taking any chances," he murmured. "I was not about to wait until tomorrow. I'm making sure I'm the first man you see after midnight."

She didn't know what to say. She didn't know what to think or feel either. She settled for a confused laugh. "It's not like I'm going to jump the first guy I see after the clock strikes."

"No, but he's going to jump you."

"What?"

"Me."

"Oh..." she breathed, rather impressed. "I see. But..."

"Can we go somewhere?" he interrupted. "I have a rental parked up the street, and I can't leave it there for long."

"Is it double-parked or something?"

"Something. Come with me?" He held out a hand and she took it. His hand sent electric sparks up her arm, and as he pulled her closer and started walking up the street she felt something like a warm magnetism emanating from him, enveloping her like a secure blanket. Almost like when he carried her.

Only her imagination?

Had it really only been ten days since she left Alaska? It seemed like forever—and Jordan looked so different. No—not exactly different—it was the setting that was wrong for him. He was the same. Almost.

She kept staring at him as she waited for him to find the keys and unlock the car. "You're looking very... neat."

"Neat?"

"Yes. Not...scruffy."

He grimaced. "Well, Simon and I do go get haircuts just before Christmas. It's one of our father-son traditions. Are you trying to tell me something about my usual appearance?"

She started smiling. "You know, when you shave, you tend to miss a spot under the right of your jaw."

"Do I?"

"And even when you do comb your hair—five minutes and it looks like someone just ruffled it good."

Jordan pulled at his hair. "It's been like that since I was six months old. I can't help it. Just ask my mom, she'll be happy to show you my baby pictures. The only way I can get it to behave is if I glue it in place with some sissy hair gel."

She giggled. "Hair gel's good—but it's not quite you, is it?" She glanced around before yanking the door open and sliding inside. "What was the hurry, anyway? You're not double-parked."

A meow answered from the back seat. Hailey gasped, then flipped the hatch of the carrier open and welcomed Helena to her lap. "Oh, my God! I missed you! Oh, Jordan, you brought her all this way?"

"She's quite a trooper. Took to the airways like a pro. Made a few friends, too."

"She's mine? I can keep her?"

"She's all yours."

"Thank you. But…"

"There's a but?"

Of course there was a but. She couldn't keep cats in her apartment. But that didn't matter now. She'd move if she had to—that had been the original plan. She'd figure something out. She wasn't losing Helena. "No. No but."

"How have you been?"

Fine was on the tip of her tongue, but then she looked into his eyes and saw he'd not been fine either. "Pretty miserable," she confessed. But only because she could see it had been the same for him. "And I miss the snow. It's funny—I've never experienced a white Christmas in my life, but now I truly miss it."

He grinned lopsidedly. "Can we take Helena to your place? She's been very considerate, but I think she might need her litter box soon."

"Did you mean what you said?"

"Which part?"

"About jumping me after midnight?"

"More or less. I suppose I could have phrased it more romantically."

She shivered. "Nah. I can live with it."

"Good."

"I missed…I miss Alaska," she whispered. "A lot."

"I… It misses you too."

"You know, it's already New Year on the east coast," she said hopefully.

"Really?"

"Yeah. Couple of hours ago, even. And in Australia it's probably been something like ten hours or more."

"But we're not on the east coast."

"Well…no."

"Or in Australia."

"No," she sighed. "I suppose we're not."

"It's just another forty minutes."

"Right. After you jump me, then what? And what exactly does jump mean, anyway?"

"You'll find out soon enough."

"When are you going back to Alaska?"

"Tomorrow. I have to be back in time for the weekend, for Simon."

She nodded. "I bet he won't be pleased to find Helena is gone."

"Don't worry. I explained. He said goodbye and asked if you'd take her surfing."

"Surfing? A cat?"

"Helena likes to hitch a ride on his sled, so he's sure she'd like surfing. I don't think he's entirely sure what surfing is."

Small talk. The air was filling up with inconsequential small talk, while inside she was bursting with all the real things that should be said.

"Well. My place?" she said, impatient, suddenly frantic to be on home turf. At home she could collect her scrambled emotions and emerge as a whole. At home she could be calm and collected and wouldn't blurt out the wrong thing or ask him stupid revealing questions like *Did you fall in love too? Is that why you're here?* Could it really be true? She was afraid to hope, afraid to ask, afraid to move past the moment—but getting home seemed urgent in order for them to move on.

Of course, an additional bonus to getting home was

that it would be midnight soon, she'd be free, and they could jump each other all they wanted without being arrested, but that was just an optional extra. The prime motivation was Helena's litter box.

"Sure. Just give me directions."

It was a short ride. The elevator ride seemed almost longer, but that was because it was filled with neighbors arriving for a party on the floor above, and she got squeezed against Jordan. He *still* smelled good. It wasn't just Alaska.

Her hand trembled as she tried to insert the key in the lock, but Jordan didn't come to her rescue. Had she trained him *too* well? Hmm. Just because a woman wanted to be independent, that didn't mean she didn't also want to be dependent—at the right time and place, of course.

Like, right here, right now.

Or at least twenty minutes from now—since he wouldn't pretend they were on the east coast or in Australia.

She showed Jordan the apartment, which took up a couple of minutes, prattled about her neighbors, asked about Simon and Mrs. Crumbs and managed to fall over her own feet and land on the living room sofa. Probably a Freudian fall, but he didn't take advantage. She gestured for him to have a seat. "Want something?"

His eyes told her what he wanted, but he just smiled. "No, thank you, I'm fine."

She looked at her watch. "Ten more minutes. Last chance if you want to make resolutions."

Jordan looked discomfited. "Right. New Year's resolutions. Are you making any?"

"Yes, a few. Not that I always keep them, but at least I'm making an effort."

"Tell me about them."

"The usual. Exercise more, call my mother more often...you know." She glanced at her watch again. "Sure you don't want a drink?"

"I'm fine."

Then silence, deep, heavy silence, and during it all she couldn't break free of the intense eye contact. There was so much unsaid, but somehow it all seemed so insignificant now.

Then finally the clock on the wall chimed midnight. Outside, cheering and fireworks ensued, but inside was silence. No Happy New Year, no clinking of champagne glasses. Just two people staring hungrily at each other, unspoken magic arching between them.

"When you left..." Jordan said at last, and she felt a flash of disappointment. Talk? What happened to *jump?* "When you said goodbye to Helena, you said you loved her. It was a wake-up call to something I'd known for a while." He leaned forward, finally breaking eye contact, but only for a moment. "See, I wanted you to say that to *me,* not the stupid cat.

"Oh..."

"Your resolution was always in the way—and it was driving me crazy, not knowing if that was the only thing in the way, or if our *vibes* were really something more than atmospheric disturbance..."

She was supposed to be saying something here, wasn't she? He'd—almost—proclaimed his love, and she wasn't saying anything. Speak, Hailey, she commanded herself, but then he sat down on the sofa next to her and that didn't help *at all.*

"You made it through your year."

"Just barely," she confessed. "And even that depends on your definition. I may have avoided relationships, but I didn't avoid…"

"What?"

"Falling in love," she muttered. This was too awkward. It wasn't supposed to be awkward. It was supposed to be blissfully romantic. She blinked away an errant tear and looked up at him, defiantly. "Enough talking. What happened to that jumping you promised me?"

He started laughing, but only for a moment because she leaned forward and caught his mouth with hers. It was warm and firm, and he responded just the way she wanted, his arms going around her, squeezing until it hurt, but she wanted it to hurt, she wanted to feel one with him, wanted the certainty of knowing he'd never let go.

He cupped her face with his hand, drew away to murmur her nickname, then his lips touched hers, gentle for a second before they both slipped under, and everything became fast and furious and full of frustration and regrets, mingled with joy and relief.

Far too soon, Jordan tore away from her, gulping in air and holding her inches and inches away even when she whimpered in protest. "You could live in Alaska, couldn't you?" he asked. "After you got lost in the forest I was afraid you'd decided you couldn't live there."

"I love Alaska," she insisted, wriggling closer. She wanted to get back to the kissing and wished he'd cooperate.

"Really?"

"Yes. I do. I just need to learn elementary survival skills before I do stupid things like go kitten hunting in the forest."

"Does that mean you'll come back to me?"

She gnawed on her lip. The problem had to be surmountable. It had to. "What about my husband?"

Jordan drew back and frowned. "Hailey, if you're going to tell me now that you really do have a husband after all…"

She hugged him, laughing. "My fictional husband. If I go back with you, how are we going to explain that to everybody?"

"That's not going to be a problem. They already know."

"*What?* They *know?*"

"Well, most people. Word is probably still spreading."

"Oh, my God. How? Who? Did you tell them?"

"Not exactly. Remember your little phone call from Robby that evening at Mrs. Crumbs' apartment?"

"Yes."

"Well, Hyacinth has Caller ID."

Hailey closed her eyes. "Are you telling me she knew already then?"

"You virtually drew two and two on the blackboard. She just added them up, and well, she's been a teacher for forty years…"

"I'll never be able to face her again. I feel so guilty about the entire thing. When she gave me Robby's sweater…" Her eyes snapped open. "She knew! She deliberately gave me Robby's sweater just to torture me!"

"Yes, she told me about that. She also said she hoped she'd gauged my size correctly."

"*Your* size? That sweater was for *you?*"

"Yep."

"She knew about us before we did?"

"Apparently so."

"And all the talk about Robby! And the cybersex and all the oil rig research…"

"She's a crafty old lady, isn't she?"

"She is in *so* much trouble… Does everybody else know too? The other teachers? Our neighbors?"

"By now, yes. Pretty much."

"Oh, God. What do they think?"

"You'd be surprised. Most of them think it's a rather good joke."

"Simon? What about Simon?"

"He was a bit confused, but I think I explained it to him well enough. That it was a sort of pretend game, and that you had good reasons for it."

"Oh, God. Poor kid. What about his mother?"

"What about her?"

"How does she feel about me lying to her child?"

"Don't worry so much, Hail. Nobody's angry. At the most they're a bit miffed that you managed to deceive them so easily. They'll get over it."

"It was so hard to leave you," she told him. "But I couldn't promise to come back. It was wrong."

"Everything's okay now, Hail. It's over. We're together."

"Know what I want to do right now?"

He grinned. "I have a pretty good idea."

"I want to go sledding," she confessed.

Jordan glanced out the window, into the warm night

filled with palm trees and traffic fumes. "Well—as much as I would like to fulfil your every wish, that one is somewhat tricky to arrange right now."

"I want to fly down the hill in darkness only lit by the northern lights and the stars and crash into the trees and be thrown off and roll around in the snow with you. I want us to end up in a tangle and start kissing and lose control..."

"And...?" Jordan prompted. "Give me the rest of the story. It's a good one."

"You know...one thing leads to another..."

"Back up a minute—one thing leads to another, but we're still outside?"

"Of course."

"In the snow? At midnight? In Alaska? In January?"

"It's a *fantasy,* Jordan!"

"I'm a practical man. When faced with a fantasy, my primary concern is how to make it come true without permanent frostbite damage to vital body parts."

She giggled. "I think this is one fantasy not meant to come true."

"Don't be hasty. It just needs a bit of adjustment. How's this? We crash—gently and on purpose of course—roll around in the snow a bit, trying our best to grope each other through six inches of clothes. Then we go back home and dive into the hot tub—and one thing leads to another."

"Hmm. Jane's hot tub?"

"Nope. The hot tub I'm installing at my place this spring."

"You're installing one?"

"Well, I have to, don't I? Fantasies are important stuff."

"Absolutely," she agreed.

"Is that a yes?"

"What was the question?"

He rolled his eyes. "Are you going to come with me back home and live happily ever after?"

"Ever after? For ever and ever and *ever?*"

"Yes. For*ever.* That's not negotiable."

She buried her face in his shoulder, unsure if the fireworks she was hearing came from outside or were a reflection of the happiness she was feeling inside. "Okay. For*ever.* I'm easy."

MILLS & BOON®

Live the emotion

SEPTEMBER 2004 HARDBACK TITLES

ROMANCE™

The Mistress Wife *Lynne Graham*	H6052	0 263 18331 9
The Outback Bridal Rescue *Emma Darcy*	H6053	0 263 18332 7
The Greek's Ultimate Revenge *Julia James*	H6054	0 263 18333 5
The Frenchman's Mistress *Kathryn Ross*	H6055	0 263 18334 3
The Billionaire's Passion *Robyn Donald*	H6056	0 263 18335 1
The Moretti Marriage *Catherine Spencer*	H6057	0 263 18336 X
The Italian's Virgin Bride *Trish Morey*	H6058	0 263 18337 8
The Wealthy Man's Waitress *Maggie Cox*	H6059	0 263 18338 6
The Australian Tycoon's Proposal *Margaret Way*	H6060	0 263 18339 4
Christmas Eve Marriage *Jessica Hart*	H6061	0 263 18340 8
The Dating Resolution *Hannah Bernard*	H6062	0 263 18341 6
The Game Show Bride *Jackie Braun*	H6063	0 263 18342 4
Fill-In Fiancée *DeAnna Talcott*	H6064	0 263 18343 2
Guess Who's Coming for Christmas? *Cara Colter*	H6065	0 263 18344 0
The Police Doctor's Secret *Marion Lennox*	H6066	0 263 18345 9
Caring For His Babies *Lilian Darcy*	H6067	0 263 18346 7

HISTORICAL ROMANCE™

The Daring Duchess *Paula Marshall*	H583	0 263 18411 0
My Lady Angel *Joanna Maitland*	H584	0 263 18412 9

MEDICAL ROMANCE™

The Doctor's Christmas Bride *Sarah Morgan*	M501	0 263 18435 8
The Recovery Assignment *Alison Roberts*	M502	0 263 18436 6

MILLS & BOON®

Live the emotion

SEPTEMBER 2004 LARGE PRINT TITLES

ROMANCE™

The Stephanides Pregnancy *Lynne Graham*
  1703 0 263 18099 9
The Passion Price *Miranda Lee* 1704 0 263 18100 6
The Sultan's Bought Bride *Jane Porter* 1705 0 263 18101 4
The Deserving Mistress *Carole Mortimer* 1706 0 263 18102 2
The Takeover Bid *Leigh Michaels* 1707 0 263 18103 0
A Marriage Worth Waiting For *Susan Fox* 1708 0 263 18104 9
The Pregnant Tycoon *Caroline Anderson* 1709 0 263 18105 7
The Honeymoon Proposal *Hannah Bernard*
  1710 0 263 18106 5

HISTORICAL ROMANCE™

A Very Unusual Governess *Sylvia Andrew* 281 0 263 18195 2
A Convenient Gentleman *Victoria Aldridge* 282 0 263 18196 0

MEDICAL ROMANCE™

Doctors in Flight *Meredith Webber* 525 0 263 18163 4
Saving Dr Tremaine *Jessica Matthews* 526 0 263 18164 2
The Spanish Consultant *Sarah Morgan* 527 0 263 18165 0
The Greek Doctor's Bride *Margaret Barker* 528 0 263 18166 9

0804 Gen Std LP

MILLS & BOON®

Live the emotion

OCTOBER 2004 HARDBACK TITLES

ROMANCE™

His Pregnancy Ultimatum *Helen Bianchin* H6068 0 263 18347 5
Bedded by the Boss *Miranda Lee* H6069 0 263 18348 3
The Brazilian Tycoon's Mistress *Fiona Hood-Stewart*
H6070 0 263 18349 1
Claiming His Christmas Bride *Carole Mortimer*
H6071 0 263 18350 5
The Mediterranean Prince's Passion *Sharon Kendrick*
H6072 0 263 18351 3
The Spaniard's Inconvenient Wife *Kate Walker* H6073 0 263 18352 1
The Italian Count's Command *Sara Wood* H6074 0 263 18353 X
Her Husband's Christmas Bargain *Margaret Mayo*
H6075 0 263 18354 8
To Win His Heart *Rebecca Winters* H6076 0 263 18355 6
The Monte Carlo Proposal *Lucy Gordon* H6077 0 263 18356 4
The Last-Minute Marriage *Marion Lennox* H6078 0 263 18357 2
The Cattleman's English Rose *Barbara Hannay*
H6079 0 263 18358 0
Santa Brought a Son *Melissa McClone* H6080 0 263 18359 9
For the Taking *Lilian Darcy* H6081 0 263 18360 2
Assignment: Christmas *Caroline Anderson* H6082 0 263 18361 0
The Police Doctor's Discovery *Laura MacDonald*
H6083 0 263 18362 9

HISTORICAL ROMANCE™

The Rake's Mistress *Nicola Cornick* H585 0 263 18413 7
An Unconventional Widow *Georgina Devon*
H586 0 263 18414 5

MEDICAL ROMANCE™

The Nurse's Wedding Rescue *Sarah Morgan*
M503 0 263 18437 4
A Doctor's Christmas Family *Meredith Webber*
M504 0 263 18438 2

0904 Gen Std HB

MILLS & BOON®

Live the emotion

OCTOBER 2004 LARGE PRINT TITLES

ROMANCE™

The Passion Bargain *Michelle Reid*	1711	0 263 18107 3
The Outback Wedding Takeover *Emma Darcy*		
	1712	0 263 18108 1
Mistress at a Price *Sara Craven*	1713	0 263 18109 X
The Billionaire Bodyguard *Sharon Kendrick*		
	1714	0 263 18110 3
Rinaldo's Inherited Bride *Lucy Gordon*	1715	0 263 18111 1
Her Stand-In Groom *Jackie Braun*	1716	0 263 18112 X
Marriage Material *Ally Blake*	1717	0 263 18113 8
The Best Man's Baby *Darcy Maguire*		
	1718	0 263 18114 6

HISTORICAL ROMANCE™

The Widow's Bargain *Juliet Landon*	283	0 263 18197 9
The Runaway Heiress *Anne O'Brien*	284	0 263 18198 7

MEDICAL ROMANCE™

Doctor at Risk *Alison Roberts*	529	0 263 18167 7
The Doctor's Outback Baby *Carol Marinelli*	530	0 263 18168 5
The Greek Children's Doctor *Sarah Morgan*	531	0 263 18169 3
The Police Surgeon's Rescue *Abigail Gordon*	532	0 263 18170 7

0904 Gen Std LP